"A visually rich, witty variation on the big-house-murder theme, displaying shades of Robert Altman's film 'Gosford Park' . . . A stylish book, ironic and fast-moving, a novel with which to have fun. Anyone seeking the definitive summer read, complete with several recipes, need look no further"
EILEEN BATTERSBY, *Irish Times*

"With it's tongue-in-cheek wit and lively characterisation, Malvaldi's novel is a delight to read . . . He has created an entertaining tale that holds the reader's attention but never takes itself too seriously"
NICK RENNISON, *B.B.C. History*

"With a host of nutjobs and dubious characters thrown into the mixture, Malvaldi has cooked up a gentle, atmospheric, Agatha-Christie-esque number with plenty of tongue-in-cheek wit and period detail in a mystery that finishes with a cute and clever twist"
JON WISE, *Weekend Sport*

Also by Marco Malvaldi in English translation

Game for Five (2014)

MARCO MALVALDI

THE ART OF KILLING WELL

Translated from the Italian by
Howard Curtis

MACLEHOSE PRESS
QUERCUS · LONDON

First published in the Italian language as *Odore di chiuso*
by Sellerio Editore in Palermo, Italy, in 2011
First published in Great Britain in 2014 by MacLehose Press
This paperback edition published in 2015 by

MacLehose Press
an imprint of Quercus Publishing Ltd
Carmelite House
50 Victoria Embankment
London EC4Y 0DZ

An Hachette UK Company

A CIP catalogue record for this book is available
from the British Library.

ISBN (PB) 978 1 78206 780 1
ISBN (Ebook) 978 1 78206 779 5

10 9 8 7 6 5 4 3 2 1

Designed and typeset in Miller Text by Libanus Press, Marlborough
Printed and bound in Great Britain by Clays Ltd, St Ives plc

To Maurizio, who played with fate
ceding it ten points;
and never losing his smile
allowed it to win.

❧

Stop the recreation, let's have some culture.

GIUSEPPE BERTOLUCCI,
from "Berlinguer, I Love You" (1997)

The beginning

The hill of San Carlo changed appearance according to the time of day.

In the morning, the sun rose behind the hills, and as the castle was built a little way below the summit, the solar rays did not directly penetrate the windows of the bedrooms housing the seventh Barone di Roccapendente, the members of his family and his guests (of whom there were usually many), which meant that they were able to sleep peacefully until quite late.

In the early afternoon, the sun's rays hit the castle, its gardens and its surrounding estate mercilessly, forcing anyone who was outside to bear a murderous heat made all the more pitiless by the humidity of the nearby marshes. But at that time, the baron and his family tended to be inside the castle, whose rooms with their vaulted ceilings were pleasantly, reassuringly cool, which helped their occupants to concentrate on card games, reading and complicated embroidery. The only people remaining outside beneath the relentless sun were the farm labourers, the estate manager, the stablemen and the gardeners, but they were accustomed to the heat.

The masters of the castle did not customarily emerge until about six in the evening, when the earth had tired of all that heat and had started to turn its back on the sun. This evening was no exception: at six o'clock on the dot, the baron and all his companions had come out into the garden to wait for the second of the guests who had been invited to enliven the weekend's hunting party. The first guest, Signor Ciceri, described on his business card as a "landscape photographer and daguerreotypist", had arrived that afternoon, to be greeted with polite indifference.

The second person due, on the other hand, was famous and quite distinguished, which was why they were waiting somewhat restlessly. Although almost all of them were wastrels who had never done an hour's honest work in their lives, the castle's residents had been subjected, thanks to the infernal heat, to a day of complete immobility in the coolness of the large rooms, and were now even more bored than usual. That was why this anticipated arrival was the genuine highlight of the day and the occupants were strolling in the garden in groups of two or three, exchanging hypotheses about the personage in question, all the while listening out for the sound of carriage wheels and horses.

There were in fact many things they did not know about the expected guest, and these things had been shared out equally among the various inquisitive groups strolling on the lawn. His personality. The way he dressed. But, above all, what he looked like. After all, this was the end of the nineteenth century, and famous people were known mainly for what they had said and done, not for what they looked like, which most of the time was completely or almost completely unknown. The good old days!

"He must be fat."

"Do you think so?"

"I'd be surprised if he wasn't. Have you ever come across a thin cook?"

"As a matter of fact, I haven't. But the man isn't actually a professional cook, is he? I gather he's a textile merchant."

"Apparently so. And that isn't his only business. I wouldn't like to . . ."

As he was thinking about what he wouldn't like to do, Lapo Bonaiuti di Roccapendente's eyes briefly met the anxious, vacuous gaze of Signorina Barbarici, nurse and companion to his grandmother, Nonna Speranza, and wondered, perhaps for the thousandth time, who would ever dream of going to bed with such a dog.

"What wouldn't you like?"

"Oh, nothing. I was miles away. Anyway, it just confirms what I was saying. A merchant who likes good food. He's a man who accumulates. Money in the bank, and fat on his belly. You'll see. They'll have to call us to prise him out of the bathtub, assuming he knows how to use one."

"What are you saying, Signorino Lapo?"

"It wouldn't surprise me. He is from Emilia-Romagna, after all. Coarse people" – he bit off the end of his cigar and spat it out – "who think only about eating, working and accumulating possessions."

Not like me, Signorino Lapo's way of walking screamed to the world: slow and aloof, his thumbs in his trouser pockets, his eyes moving from side to side. New clothes, English walking boots.

Lapo's vision of the way to behave with other human beings was simple and uncomplicated. If she was a woman and beautiful, you went to bed with her. If she was a woman and ugly, you went to bed with a different woman. If he was a man, you went to the brothel together. Everything else in life – eating, chatting, riding, and the occasional hunting party – was the moral obligation of a genuine man of the world, who had to rub shoulders with everyone, even inferior beings like Signorina Barbarici: a kind of interlude which, when pleasant, made the waiting less tiresome and, when unpleasant, added a little urgency to the great moment.

Signorina Barbarici did not reply. But then she had not been asked for her opinion.

Signorina Barbarici's relationship with the world was also quite well defined: she was afraid. Of everything.

Storms, for example. Brigands, who came into your house, stole your jewellery and your embroidered tablecloths and did terrible things to women. Bees, which got in everywhere and after they had stung you stayed there, clinging stupidly to their target, and you had to get them off you. Her father, who was forever yelling. Her mother, who bore the brunt of it and passed it on to her. Men. Women. Solitude.

That was why Signorina Barbarici (who had been christened Annamaria some decades earlier: rather a pointless act, because nobody ever called her by her name) had, in order to survive, transformed herself into a kind of machine that agreed with everything. Only this ability made it possible for her to bear without serious consequences the daily humiliations she suffered at the hands of Signora Speranza. At the moment, though, for the first time that day, the signora was ignoring her and talking to her granddaughter in a sundrenched corner.

~~❧~~

"He's not going to cook for us, is he?"

"I have no idea, Nonna."

"Because I've never eaten anything that wasn't made by Parisina. A man, can you imagine? Since when have men taken to cooking, I ask you?"

"Many great cooks have been men, Nonna. Vatel, for example. Brillat-Savarin."

"I've never heard of them. And you've only read about them in books. I don't suppose you've ever eaten anything cooked by this Brillassavèn. Like me, you've always eaten what Parisina makes. Though even she, lately . . . Well, let's not go into that, shall we? I may be old, but I'm not stupid. Apparently, there's no such thing as meat these days. Fish only on Friday, otherwise anchovies. Endless vegetables. We've become goats, that's what we've become."

She was indeed old. And she had good reason to complain: she was in a wheelchair, and had not been able to move around for years. Not that it could have been much easier before, given that she must have weighed a good hundred kilos, badly distributed, from the neck down, over a useless body. But her face was thin, and her jaw still worked perfectly well, especially when she opened it to speak.

"It's summer, Nonna, and very hot. We should eat light food."

"Summer my foot. What do you care, all of you? The less you

give me to eat, the sooner I'll die, and you'll have one less thing to worry about. Away with the old lady! She's so fat, it might cost a bit to bury her, but then you'll have more room."

"Nonna, people are coming."

That was the only way to shut her up: decorum before everything. And Cecilia knew that. Which was another reason she did not fit into this household.

Cecilia was short, with plump hands and hair gathered in a plait. Her body required a little imagination, given that she was trapped inside a dress that was a cross between a monk's habit and a grain silo. Just as well, since her strong point was her eyes. Two large dark eyes flecked with green, whose calm, frank, direct gaze told you that she knew perfectly well you hadn't changed your underwear this morning, but that when it came down to it, that was your affair.

～ゞ～

Remote from these various debates, the baron was waiting at the top of the garden for a sign from Teodoro, his invaluable butler. As he waited for Teodoro to announce, simply by changing position, that the guest's arrival was imminent, the baron wondered where he would be right now without Teodoro.

Unaware of this, the butler elegantly scanned the bend in the road beyond the chestnut tree. He was wearing his gloves, his livery and his bow tie: to all appearances, he was fastidiously dressed. In reality, beneath this exterior, Teodoro was wearing only a dicky, cut off at the sleeves and halfway down the back, with just enough of it left not to stain his jacket with sweat, which was also why he was not wearing any socks, vest or long johns, a trick he employed during the summer, and which afforded him a keen satisfaction.

❦

". . . and it was delicious, really delicious! And digestible, too, even though it had nutmeg, which I really can't digest and always comes up into my throat, and in fact in the book he says you should be careful with spices because they can be unpleasant for ladies, but in fact . . ."

If one had to describe the two ladies sitting at the small wrought-iron table, one would have to start with the buttons. The first one's cotton dress was done up at the back by a close-packed line of round buttons, the last of which was situated just one millimetre beneath the third cervical vertebra, like a mother-of-pearl garrotte. There were similar lines of buttons on the sleeves, from elbow to wrist, and on the half-boots, from calf to knee (if anyone had been able to see her calves or her knees). From the way she spoke and how she was dressed, it was safe to say that breathing was not a necessity for this woman.

". . . that among other things poor Bastiana also made pigeon that way, but she overcooked it and it always ended up as tough as wood, and poor Ettore was the one who had to eat it and even say it was good, God help us, otherwise she would call him mad, even though she herself was never exactly normal, you remember Bastiana, don't you? Of course you do, poor thing . . ."

The other lady was wearing a flowered dress, with gold braid down the front, from neck to shin, to protect her substantial bosom from the rays of the sun. Her wizened little head was nodding rhythmically. The only way she could possibly have got a word in edgeways would have been to have hit her companion over the head with her chair, and so her contribution to the debate was limited to a few sporadic squeaks.

It was obvious that they were sisters, and equally obvious that they were spinsters: a slow, inexorable and bitter destiny which, apart from marking them out in their lives and in their clothing, had also affected their official designation. According to the register of births, the two women were Cosima and Ugolina Bonaiuti Ferro, first cousins to the baron, but, for everyone else, including the servants, they were simply "the old maids".

They lived a parallel life, made up of embroidery, reading out loud and much pointless stroking of Briciola, the bilious Yorkshire terrier which had been sold to the baron as a hunting dog and adopted by the two sisters when the baron, after one look at it, had kicked it away, muttering that with such a dog the only thing you might just possibly be able to hunt would be mice.

~~~

A cookery book. Poor Italy.

Walking slowly at a safe distance from the two ladies and their chatter, his feet on the lawn and his mind just back from Parnassus, Signorino Gaddo was reflecting despite himself on the supposed merits of the awaited guest. In this atmosphere, there was no point even mentioning poetry.

You're going to be pleased, his father had said to him. A first-rate man of letters will be coming here for the boar hunt, so for once you'll have someone of your own level and may even deign to open your mouth a little.

Gaddo had greeted the news with apparent equanimity, but things had started to boil up inside him.

Some time earlier he had gathered together his best poems, tied them with a red ribbon, and put them in an elegant cardboard cylinder. Not many, because genius is a question of detail, of phrasing, not of weight: it is the spark that lights the fire, not the log. It had been a difficult choice, of course, and hard-won. It had cost him a great deal to exclude some of his favourite verses, such as "Impetuous Heart", and, even today, he was haunted by the possibility that he had made a mistake and had been too drastic. But so be it. The selection had been made, the cylinder had been sealed and stamped and sent off, with the most elegant of letters of presentation, to the Great Poet, to whom his own region, the Maremma, had given birth, a fact that the rest of Italy could only envy.

Giosue Carducci.

After which he had waited feverishly for the result of that fit of enthusiasm. Many was the time he had fantasised about the form of the message – a note, a letter, even an invitation to the Great Poet's house in Bolgheri – through which his art would begin to be recognised and at last take flight.

Never once, not even when he was filled with vermouth, had he dared hope for a visit.

But when his father had spoken those words, his heart had begun to beat faster, as befitted a sensitive soul, and his brain had told him that the great moment had arrived.

A man of letters coming to Roccapendente. He had not even asked the name, so certain was he. Who else could it be but the Great Poet?

In the course of the evening, he had toyed with the image of the Great Poet, seated behind his chestnut desk (all poets must have chestnut desks, on pain of disqualification), absorbed in reading one of his, Gaddo's, poems and nodding with approval, happy at last to have found an heir worthy of his fame.

And now it turned out that Gaddo had been mistaken.

The famous man of letters who would be visiting the castle was not Giosue Carducci at all.

As if that were not bad enough, he wasn't even a poet.

A novelist, he had thought.

Worse still.

The man of letters about to enjoy the tranquillity and hospitality of Roccapendente was someone who had written a *cookery book*.

It was enough to make one beat one's head against the wall.

❧

All at once, the baron saw Teodoro rise to his full height and his eyes turn in a westerly direction. This was not a chance movement: from the bend in the road beyond the chestnut tree came a swirling cloud of dust, followed after a moment by a small trap driven by a bare-headed man and drawn by a horse that had seen better days.

Sitting in the trap, looking about him, was a man with a large pair of mutton-chop whiskers. From this distance it was impossible to say more, given that the only things so far distinguishable were those beautiful white whiskers, which stood out in spite of the dust and the distance.

As the trap approached, the residents gathered on the patio in front of the veranda, ready to greet the newcomer, and the baron watched as Teodoro walked to the spot where the trap would stop, in order to take the guest's luggage.

The trap came to a halt.

The coachman got down, adjusted his jacket, opened the door with a somewhat coarse gesture, and a robust foot pressed heavily on the step. In one hand the guest held a book, the cover of which bore an English title, and in the other a wicker basket containing two of the fattest cats ever seen. He was wearing a frock coat and a top hat. Between his whiskers, a broad, good-natured smile could be made out.

No sooner had he got off than Teodoro cleared his throat and, in a distinct voice, recited his greeting:

"Signor Pellegrino Artusi, welcome to Roccapendente."

Friday, seven in the evening

It was dinner time at the castle. And this evening, as always when there were visitors, dinner was served in the so-called Olympus Room.

If the baron and his dinner guests had raised their eyes, they would have had the opportunity to admire the wonderful frescoes of Jacopuccio da Campiglia, a painter known to posterity for having frescoed the entire castle of Roccapendente and even better known to his contemporaries for the incredible number of debts incurred in the taverns and wine shops of the Val di Cornia. It was on this ceiling, where the gods of Olympus chased one another in an eternal, motionless race, that Jacopuccio had given the best of himself, and while Heracles crushed the lion, Orpheus moved the stones to tears and Zeus seduced Aphrodite (pictorial licence, of course: good old Jacopuccio could barely read), they all watched tirelessly over the master of Roccapendente and his family – who, for their part, heads down and jaws going at full tilt, were tearing apart a fish pie of colossal dimensions and completely ignoring all that beauty.

～≈～

The one eating slowly was the baron, who must have gazed admiringly at that ceiling a thousand times, without ever tiring of it – but when there was something to eat, you ate.

꙳

The one eating listlessly was Gaddo, who might have the sensitivity of spirit to appreciate beauty but was now busy casting sidelong glances at the self-styled man of letters as the latter stuffed himself with pie, his white whiskers moving up and down in time to the rhythm of his jaws.

꙳

The one eating briskly and noisily was Lapo, who preferred beautiful things of flesh and blood rather than on walls, and was now watching his sister and thinking that if she didn't dress like a penitent she might almost look like a woman, and then it might actually be possible to find her a husband and get her out of his hair – with that female arrogance of hers, she was always finding fault with him.

꙳

The one eating with small bites was Cecilia, who was looking curiously at the bewhiskered guest and completely ignoring Lapo's bovine gaze and his all too obvious thoughts (if you could call them that). Men never understood that women were able to guess what they were thinking from their behaviour, the look in their eyes, the way they were sitting, and so on. This was true of all men, let alone Lapo, who had all the intelligence of a fruit bowl. Signor Artusi, on the other hand, was eating away in silence, completely engrossed, clearly savouring every mouthful. He seemed like someone who thought about what he was doing, and Cecilia liked that.

The one who would have been eating Parisina's excellent pie was Nonna Speranza, if age and illness had not taken away her appetite and this family of good-for-nothings had not taken away the high spirits we all begin to lose even when we are young. Horses, women, poetry! The only one of her grandchildren with a modicum of brains was unfortunate enough to have been born a woman. As unfortunate as she herself was, confined by a body she had not chosen within a family she would never have chosen if she had had any choice in the matter.

The one eating without thinking anything at all was Signor Ciceri, his jaw rotating slowly without in any way modifying his smile. In fact, Fabrizio Ciceri rarely lost his smile, and never his appetite.

And last but not least, the one eating with gusto was the be-whiskered guest, sometimes with his eyes closed. Partly to savour that divine pie, and partly not to feel the eyes of the other dinner guests on him: he had no desire to be overcome once again by that shyness which had always afflicted him in the houses of strangers, a shyness which nobody would ever have guessed at, looking at his hair as rigid as King Umberto's and his military whiskers.

"So, Dottore Artusi, what do you think of my food?"

Sitting at the head of the table, the baron was visibly satisfied. At first, he had seen Artusi serve himself parsimoniously and eat slowly, in small bites, chewing a lot, even though fish pie by its very nature is easy to swallow: the typical demeanour of someone who eats out of duty.

By the third portion, he had changed his mind. Clearly, Artusi was a long-distance runner, not a sprinter: slow, methodical, steady, relentless. When Teodoro had asked him, "Would the signore like some?" for the third time, he had almost drawn the tray to himself. One never serves oneself three times from the same dish. It is bad manners. It gives the impression that one is only there to eat. But the gleam in the guest's eyes had told him that they might have to use a shovel.

Now, Artusi had the placid expression of someone who has removed the wrinkles from his stomach, and the satisfied expression of someone who has eaten really well, and he had no need to be tactful in answering the baron's question.

"Excellent, Barone, excellent," he said, as Teodoro carried away the dish. "I know very little about pies, but this, if you'll allow me, was superb. And exceedingly well prepared. In fact, I have a favour to ask you."

"I think I know what it is. But I'm not the one you should ask. If you like, I can send for the cook immediately."

"I'm most grateful. I should be even more so if I were allowed to go to the kitchen in person."

The baron was rendered speechless for a moment.

"You see," Artusi continued, blushing, "the dish we have just tasted is actually quite complex. As you will have gathered, I should like to include it in my little treatise on the art of good food. But in order to reproduce this delicacy correctly, and make sure that my twenty readers can do the same, I need, I fear, to have things explained to me in the greatest detail."

"So you personally tell your cook what to do?" asked Lapo.

"Not exactly," replied Artusi. "The first time I get ready to make a dish, I try it out myself. Then, when I am sure of the quantities and the procedure, I pass it to my cook."

"So your wife never cooks."

"Alas, I'm not married, Signorino Lapo."

From the corner where the old maids sat came a brief, breathless little laugh.

"As I was saying, I need to have everything explained in great detail, and I fear that for others the conversation would be somewhat tedious."

You can bet your whiskers on that, said Lapo's facial expression.

The baron, though, smiled. "I thank you for that thought. If you would like to stay with us for dessert and coffee, Teodoro will then show you to the kitchen."

"I am most grateful."

"I hope, however, that you do not linger there for too long, given that we will then be moving into the billiard room to toast our health. Books are useful, but food and drink are necessities, are they not?"

～※～

"Talking of books," Nonna Speranza said, "I noticed that you have rather a strange one with you."

The dessert and the coffee had arrived in the meantime. The dessert was a fresh cheesecake on a base of crumbled butter biscuits, decorated with blueberries and raspberries, and had immediately been polished off by the dinner guests – which was why the coffee was now a necessity.

The problem was the cup.

When one has whiskers that are thick, drooping, and two centimetres long, not all glasses and cups are as easy to negotiate. The cup Artusi had in front of him, for example, posed the problem of how to drink the coffee without dipping his precious whiskers in the restorative liquid. While he was studying the situation, he replied, "Ah, so you noticed?"

"It would have been difficult not to," Gaddo said in a tone which, some seventy years later, would have made him a senior officer in the Stasi. "The cover was in exceptionally bad taste."

"You should never judge a book by its cover, Gadduccio," Cecilia said amiably.

"And you should never speak unless you are spoken to, my dear Cecilia," replied Lapo without looking at her. "You're a young lady now, and there are certain things you ought to know. I believe—"

"Oh, don't interfere in discussions about books, Lapo," Cecilia cut in. "It doesn't suit you. If and when the conversation moves on to the subject of how to fritter away money, we'll let you know."

"Cecilia!" cried her grandmother, also without looking at her. That was all she had to say. After waiting for a moment to make sure that her granddaughter had calmed down, she went on, "If

I have understood correctly, it is a book about criminal investigations."

In the meantime, Artusi had brought the operation to a satisfactory conclusion, knocking back the coffee while keeping his whiskers surprisingly clean, thanks to the so-called "anteater method" (mouth like a trumpet, lips extended, a quick – and, as far as possible, silent – sucking movement, and so on) so dear to the owners of whiskers in the Western world.

"That is indeed the case," Artusi said, putting his cup down, then, as if to apologise for possessing such a uncommon book, "I got it from the English bookseller in the Via de' Cerretani."

Seeing that everyone had fallen silent, Artusi continued, more to fill the embarrassed silence that descends when people do not know each other well than out of any desire to inform the dinner guests, "The main character is a Londoner of private means. Highly intelligent, physically strong and with a cast-iron memory. A trifle eccentric, like many Englishmen. A great violinist, according to the narrator, and prone to all kinds of excesses to escape boredom. Morphine, opium and suchlike, much to the annoyance of the man with whom he shares a flat, a highly respectable doctor."

"And this man finds himself involved in a crime?"

"On the contrary. This fellow seeks out crimes. That is his element, like the sea for fish. He reads the newspapers, asks the police for information, even performs experiments to determine whether such and such a stain is indeed blood and not rust or some other substance. And when he is quite sure as to how a crime was committed, he goes to the police and tells them what they must do and whom to arrest. He describes himself as a private investigator."

"Third-rate literature," Gaddo said, "made to satisfy the tastes of coarse people. Corpses, sensational events, half-naked women and other obscenities. Fit only for servant girls, or merchants."

As the baron changed colour, becoming slightly purple, there was heard the croaky voice of Signorina Ferro (Cosima, to be exact – not that it is necessary, because the other old maid never speaks): "Surely the signore is a merchant, am I not right? And even quite well known in his city."

"The fact is, Signorina Cosima," stammered Artusi, his cheeks also somewhat inflamed, "I have been blessed by fate. My father left me a prosperous business, and I have simply followed in his footsteps. Alone, believe me, I wouldn't have succeeded at anything. Everything I have I owe to my parents."

"It is rather the same with us nobles," Nonna Speranza said. "One inherits a title and uses it all one's life, even if one is a good-for-nothing who cannot do a single thing except write poems."

It was Gaddo's turn to grow purple, and Lapo who now spoke up: "And what kind of business are you involved in, Signor Artusi, if you don't mind my asking?"

"Textiles, mainly. Silk, brocades, Oriental fabrics. Sometimes also clothes or tapestries, but not very often."

"I see. I seem to recall you also act as a money changer or banker."

"I fear you're mistaken, Signorino Lapo. It is a reputation that has followed me for some time, but it is entirely undeserved, believe me."

"Well, Dottore Artusi," the baron cut in, "if you want to see the cook, I think now is the best moment. Our servants are accustomed to retiring early and rising with the sun."

"Which is all to the good. It's the only way, in my opinion, to lead a healthy life. For the moment I thank you for this delicious dinner, the secret of which I hope shortly to discover." Artusi laughed behind his whiskers in a forced attempt at humour. "To be quite honest, I can't promise that I'll be able to keep you company in your toast. It was a long, tiresome journey, and I'm starting to be of an age when certain efforts exact their price. I therefore wish you a happy toast, and a good night."

"Goodnight to you, and thank you for your company," the baron said, visibly relieved.

From the diary of Pellegrino Artusi

Friday, 16 June, 1895

Arrived safe and sound at the castle of Roccapendente.

The castle is beautiful, but the interior strikes me as unusually devoid of furnishings, although it may be the sheer size of the rooms and staircases that gives me that impression.

As far as beauty of appearance is concerned, even the servants are well suited to the castle. I was conducted to my room by a young lady of some twenty years, so tall and of such proud features that I suspected she might originally be from Scandinavia; but, as she preceded me up the stairs, I was able to appreciate her way of wiggling her assets, which appeared to me to be totally Latin.

I am now of an age when the pleasures of the flesh are those which can be savoured hot from the oven, rather than those involving the heat of passion: which is why I myself was surprised, seeing my guide swaying in front of me, to sense the reawakening of feelings I had long thought dulled.

The Pellegrino of not a few years ago, reaching the door of his room, would have closed it behind him and with his best smile, sure of what he was doing, would have taken advantage, in every sense of the term, of the hospitality of the house. The Pellegrino of today, having noted the softness of the bed and the quilt, dismissed the maid, asking her to send up the manservant to unpack my luggage; as I did so, I managed to snatch a fleeting caress, which even I thought was pathetic, of those fine marmoreal hips.

Even the manservant who helped me with my luggage was a young Adonis, tall and proud and bright-eyed, although decidedly talkative for a servant; during the half-hour it took him to lay out my few garments, he several times took the liberty of addressing me. It was thus that I received various pieces of information which I could easily have done without, such as the fact that he could not stand asparagus and courgettes (which would be served at dinner) and that he had never tasted fish (of which there would be a dish). He was even kind enough to inform me that, if I liked making sporting bets on the horses, or on the players of bracciale, I could if I so wished avail myself of his services to place the bet, a task he regularly performed for the baron and his guests. It was a pointless offer, given that I do not usually throw away my money on bets, a fact of which he was of course unaware. In conclusion, as if he had not already done enough to break my tommasei, he had the bad grace to take the basket where Bianchino and Sibillone were now fast asleep and slam it unceremoniously on the chest of drawers, as if, instead of two little animals, it contained potatoes. Already shaken by the journey, my two cats did not appreciate that at all, and immediately hid under the bed, from where, with much hissing, they refused my offers of food and cuddles. Tonight, coming back from the kitchen, I had to win them over with a little of the tuna pie which was served to us at dinner, and which I had managed, with some difficulty, to put aside; now, as I write, they are both curled up in the middle of the bedspread, purring with satisfaction.

※

I hope to be able to delight them again with this delicacy when I am back in Florence. But I have to admit that I do not know how likely that is, after the rather singular manner in which the cook explained the recipe to me.

I thought I had made a wise move in asking if I could go myself to the kitchen instead of having the cook brought to the dining room, since I have often noted that members of the servant class are reluctant to speak in front of their masters. They do not find it easy to express themselves, and the presence of persons of high birth embarrasses them.

This little woman, on the other hand, proved as gifted with words as she must be little gifted with brain. I was greeted as one might greet a coalman, and was ordered to remain by the door until she had finished doing whatever it was she was doing; and, even after that, I remained by the door, inclined as I was to accept any small madness just to see the procedure for making that delicacy revealed.

Unfortunately, the woman overwhelmed me with a barely comprehensible explanation, which I shall attempt to transcribe here literally:

"Alright, then, you use only the whites of the celery and put them in a pan with the olives and the peppers, but not green olives, and not even those big black ones; the best are the red olives, but you hardly ever find them and so you make do with the tiny black

29

ones. *After you've put in the bread and the tuna, you heat it until you see it's ready, but make sure it is ready; or rather, make sure the bread is put in the milk when it's boiling hot, otherwise it doesn't take at all. Then you break two eggs and beat them, and put everything in the oven with the breadcrumbs, and then take it out after a while."*

As she was telling me all this, I did not understand a thing; but I consoled myself with the thought that it would appear clearer to me when I reread it.

Now, reading over what I have written, all I feel is dismay.

Who knows? Perhaps the night will bring enlightenment; but I have to say that having developed a taste for that dish, it seems likely to remain unsatisfied.

❧

All this has made the evening all the more bitter, given that the dinner itself was not especially pleasant. Not because of the food, of course, since that old bat with the bonnet proved to be a true expert in her art; but rather, because of my companions at the table.

The baron was as gracious as always, as if we were at Montecatini taking the waters; but over the rest of the family, if this were a letter and not a diary, it would be appropriate to draw a veil. One of the two sons, Gaddo, seems to hate me for no apparent reason. But at least he limits himself to sarcasm, which is more than can be said for his younger brother, who has accused me almost openly of being a usurer. As for the distaff side, the baron's daughter is probably not a bad person, but I fear she is much too *clever for the rest of the family, except perhaps for the dowager baroness, Speranza, who sends shivers down one's spine at the mere sight of her; then there are the two old maids of the family – there always have to be old maids in these places – together with their dog, a snarling ball of fur to which I have already been forced to administer a few good kicks in order to keep it away from my trousers.*

Given the circumstances, the atmosphere at the dinner table was not idyllic, and after my visit to the kitchen I preferred to retire, which was not the case with the castle's other guest, Signor Ciceri, who has been invited here to photograph the baron and his family, and who seems to me the classic upstart peasant in gentleman's clothes.

To sum up, I came here to relax and spend a few quiet days, and it seems that I will have to find that quiet by myself. Let us hope things improve tomorrow, and that we have good hunting!

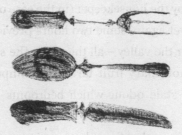

Saturday, early morning

There are many ways to wake up in the morning.

At the castle of Roccapendente, for example, the servants were awakened by the crowing of a cock, the one creature enthused by the fact that once again the sun had managed to roll up over the mountains. Among them were some who did not hear, or who pretended not to hear, that stupid bird: they were roused to a vertical position by the estate manager, good old Amidei, who was always happy to give a good kick in the backside to those who were not awake or quick enough.

A quite different awakening was reserved for the baron and the other residents, who were usually notified by Teodoro (in the case of the men) or by the housekeeper (in the case of the women) that this morning, yet again, some two hours previously, the sun had peeped out over the valley – all this while the smell of coffee and Parisina's extraordinary fruit tarts easily imposed itself on the dense, vaguely stale odour which bedrooms have early in the morning.

Be that as it may, that Saturday morning presented something quite unscheduled: because never before had either the residents or the servants been awakened by the kind of bloodcurdling scream that had just startled the castle.

The inhuman scream was the doing of Signorina Barbarici, who was lying face down on the ground outside a small door of wood and iron in the basement. The poor woman was not only motionless, she had fainted, as is only fitting for a woman in a novel set at the end of the nineteenth century.

Those not new to the castle would no doubt have known that the small door was that of the cellar, and that as such it was situated in the part of the castle used by the servants. What they might not have known was that the small room adjoining the larger room from which you could enter the cellar itself, and which was the coolest room in the house, served as a refuge for Teodoro the butler, who often retired there to read at those times when his services were not required. The masters only rarely descended to this part of the castle, and in fact it had been Parisina the cook and the other kitchen staff who had found the signorina and administered first aid. Given the situation, Parisina had immediately dispatched someone to the kitchen to fetch vinegar to revive the poor lady, after which she had turned Signorina Barbarici onto her back and had begun to give her a few timid slaps. That was all that was needed for the signorina to reopen her eyes, much to the displeasure of Parisina, who would have gladly increased the intensity of her slaps, because thanks to the fright she had been given by this idiot's screaming, a pan with six eggs for Signorino Lapo's zabaglione had fallen to the floor and now she would have to start all over again.

Once she had recovered, the signorina was made to sit down and comforted with a nice glass of alchermes. When her face had turned almost pink again, Parisina asked her with the courtesy obliged by their difference in status, "Are you alright, signorina?"

Signorina Barbarici nodded to indicate yes as she swallowed the alchermes.

"Did something frighten you, signorina?"

Probably her own shadow, thought the entire servant body.

Without showing annoyance at the obvious emphasis with which the cook called her "signorina", the woman again nodded and pointed to the reinforced door.

～➳≪～

Some time later, the dowager baroness was woken by a housemaid as white as a sheet. Not exactly woken, more like exposed to the light, given that a) the baroness never slept very much and b) even if she had slept, the feral scream produced by her nurse a little while earlier would have woken even the bedspread.

Sure enough, as the housemaid pulled back the curtains, the old lady asked acidly, "What on earth was that squawking earlier?"

"Er . . . Signorina Barbarici, Baronessa. She had a terrible fright."

"Ah, I see, Barbarici had a fright," the baroness said with a sigh. "Just as well. That'll keep her quiet for a while."

The housemaid had not replied, obviously, but instead of withdrawing from the room with a curtsey she had remained there, with her feet converging and her hands tightly clasped. The dowager baroness was not accustomed to regarding the members of the staff as actual human beings, which was why she continued in a bitter tone, without looking at the girl, "And what happened, pray, to give the idiot a fright?"

"She says she saw a dead body in the cellar, Baronessa."

"Are you sure, signorina?"

Signorina Barbarici, uncomfortable at being the centre of attention, had nodded fervently in answer to the baron's question, all the while continuing to look down at the floor as if she herself were responsible for the supposed body in the cellar. Around her stood all the occupants of the castle, from the baron down to the lowliest of the scullery maids – apart from the estate manager, who by now was already in the fields supervising the labourers, and Lapo, who had gone down to the village the previous evening and must have lingered in the brothel with his debauched friends.

"And why on earth did you close the cellar door?"

"What?"

"The cellar door, my dear. That door is always open. Why on earth did you close it? Was it really so frightful?"

Basically, the baron wanted to know what sight awaited him beyond the door. That Signorina Barbarici had seen something, there could be no doubt. What he wanted to know was whether, before opening the door, he should dismiss all those present in order to spare them a horrific spectacle. But the signorina looked at him like a startled dog. "I didn't close anything, Barone," she said. "The door was already closed."

"What?"

"The . . . the door, as I said. I even tried to open it, but . . ."

"So how did you manage to see what's inside?"

The poor woman turned as red as a watermelon (the inside of a watermelon, of course, otherwise she would have turned green) and uttered something like ". . . ole". Nobody understood. At the third attempt, a complete sentence emerged:

"I looked through the keyhole."

Consternation. Anything might have been expected of Signorina Barbarici except that she would take to looking through other people's keyholes. Once a few moments had passed, the questions came thick and fast.

"Through the keyhole?"

"What on earth made you think of looking through the keyhole?"

"Why did you try to open the cellar door?"

"What were you doing awake at half past six in the morning?"

Before the chronological progression of the questions reached the point of asking her how she could ever have taken the liberty of being born (a question she often asked herself anyway) the baron raised a hand to demand silence. Having obtained it, he looked at Signorina Barbarici.

"I wake up early in the morning," she said. "I walk around the castle while everybody is asleep. I like it."

She omitted to explain that this was the only opportunity she had to spend an hour alone without the dowager baroness breathing down her neck.

"I walk along the corridors, down the stairs, into the cellar . . . it's nice and quiet . . . everything's always the same. But this morning, the cellar door was closed. It's usually open."

Here, too, the good signorina passed over the fact that what attracted her to the cellar was not so much the peace and quiet as the bottles of absinthe that Signorino Gaddo had brought from Paris six months earlier, extolling it as the liquor of the poets, the drink of perdition, only to then leave the bottles untouched in the cellar after taking a sip and deciding that the French poets were as depraved in their palates as in everything else. The poor lady had in fact got into the habit of serving herself a decent glass of the stuff in the course of her morning walks, finding it a great help in putting up with the dowager baroness.

"Except that this morning the door was closed, and I couldn't open it. So I—"

"So you, instead of walking past, took the opportunity to look through the keyhole to see if by any chance Teodoro was in his underwear on the other side of the door," said Lapo, who had joined the company in the meantime: the only person dressed in evening clothes in the middle of all these people in their dressing gowns, and obviously blind drunk. "Isn't that right, you old sow?"

"Lapo," the baron said through clenched jaws, "please go to your room."

"Why? I get the impression everyone is having a great time here."

In the silence that followed, Signorina Barbarici began weeping softly.

"Lapo, you're drunk," Gaddo tried to say.

"Oh, well, I'm not the only one. Just smell this Peeping Tom here. She stinks of alchermes. In my opinion—"

"LAPO!"

"Alright, alright, general. I'll be good. I only want to know what's going on."

Ignoring him, Signorina Barbarici resumed through her tears, "I looked and saw something, and I couldn't tell [sob], I couldn't tell what it was. Then I realised it was a hand. But it was white [sob], as white as . . . a corpse . . ."

At this point, the signorina broke down completely.

"I see," the baron said solemnly. Then he stepped away from the whimpering woman and addressed his guests. "I do beg your pardon for this unfortunate mishap. I think it's now clear what happened. The butler must have fallen asleep in the cellar, with the bolt drawn, and did not notice that day had dawned. Signorina Barbarici saw a hand dangling, and being of a nervous and impressionable nature concluded that she had seen a corpse."

"Do you really think so?" asked Signor Ciceri, who looked even fatter in his cotton dressing gown and nightshirt.

"It wouldn't be the first time he's done something like this, unfortunately," the baron said, looking at the door. "Now, if you'll excuse me—"

"Forgive me, father," Gaddo said, "but I fear Signor Ciceri meant something else."

"I thank you, Signorino Gaddo. Barone, I'm afraid that before opening that door we have to send the ladies away and steel ourselves for a tragic spectacle. I'm a heavy sleeper, and if the signorina's scream woke even me, lying upstairs . . ."

The baron seemed to think this over for a few moments, even though there was not really much to think about.

He, too, had been startled from his sleep by the poor woman's bellowing, after a horrible night filled with palpitations and frightful stomach pains. Signorina Barbarici's scream had been positively bloodcurdling, and had awakened the whole castle. Whoever the hand behind that door belonged to, the poor fellow was either dead or deaf. And as the baron well knew, Teodoro had excellent hearing.

In the silence, Signor Ciceri resumed, "Is this door the only way to gain access to the room?"

The baron and Gaddo said yes simultaneously. Gaddo looked at his father, who said quietly, "You're right. Gentlemen, I think the best thing we can do is open this blasted door."

❧

Obviously, by "open" the baron meant "have opened by someone able to do so": the baron could hardly be expected to put his own diaphanous, manicured hands to work, nor could Gaddo, who found it an effort to hold a pen, be expected to pick up a hammer and chisel.

In such matters, there was a precise hierarchy to be observed. In the first place, you called the estate manager, who in turn would call whichever of the servants seemed to him most fitted to the task and would supervise him as he worked, all under the watchful gaze of the family and guests, including the dowager baroness who had had herself brought down for that very purpose.

One hour later, supervised and scrutinised by a multitude of eyes, the worker selected (Amedeo Farini, son of the late Crescenzo, known as "the cat" because of his astounding ability to sleep anything from sixteen to twenty hours a day) gave the final hammer blow and the hinges of the reinforced door yielded, after which he stood up and leaned all his weight on the door in order to bend it sufficiently for it to open. Which it did, noisily. Cautiously, the baron entered. As if by tacit agreement, he was immediately followed by the men, one at a time. A glance was enough for everyone. There was no doubt about it: Teodoro was dead.

For those morbid readers who love detailed descriptions, let us say that the body was slumped on a wicker chair, with one hand dangling and remarkably pale, unlike his face which was a reddish purple. Teodoro's work jacket had been placed carefully on a coathanger. On a small table in front of the dead man was a tray with a bottle of port and a glass with a little red wine.

The room was pervaded by a strange smell.

After entering, the baron stood to one side and avoided looking at the body. He was already as white as a sheet because of his sleepless night, but now he was giving even the corpse a run for his money. Gaddo stood beside him with his hand on his shoulder. Lapo, having at last realised the gravity of the situation, was close to the wall, motionless, trying to cause as little disturbance as possible. Signor Ciceri had knelt by the body and was gravely scrutinising the face. In short, everyone was behaving normally.

Everyone except Artusi. After walking about the room for a while with a solemn frown befitting those who have found a corpse, he had begun to sniff the air in a manner that was first curious, then methodical.

In the meantime, Signor Ciceri had got to his feet. "A heart attack, I fear. Barone, is there a doctor in the vicinity of the castle?"

The baron pulled himself together. "What? No, no. The nearest doctor is in the village, in Campiglia Marittima. I'll go and fetch him immediately."

"Do you feel up to it? You seem quite shaken."

"Really, father," Gaddo said. "You look very tired. Perhaps I could—"

"Thank you, Gaddo, but no. I'll go."

"At least let me go with you," Signor Ciceri said with a slight smile. "With my trap we'll do it in a flash."

The baron thought this over for a moment. He was clearly none too enthusiastic about the idea. Then he shook his head and sighed, "If you insist, I'm most grateful. Gaddo, call Amidei and have him get Signor Ciceri's trap ready."

Gaddo did not reply: he was looking at Artusi, eyes wide with astonishment.

With good reason, in fact. Because Artusi, after sniffing the whole room, had gone over to the night table, taken out a full chamber pot, and now, with an intrigued air, was carefully sniffing the contents.

Fortunately, the baron had not noticed. Still looking elsewhere, he repeated, "Gaddo, please."

Gaddo shook himself, and gave a forced smile. "I'm sorry, father. I'm going right now."

41

Saturday, lunchtime

Until lunchtime, the morning had been sad but peaceful.

After the grim awakening, the residents of the castle had drifted outside in small groups, making sure they stayed away until the doctor arrived with the undertakers to take away the mortal remains, and eagerly awaiting lunch, which was, of course, their favourite pastime.

The Bonaiuti Ferro sisters had gone to ground in the little chapel close to the woods and there, kneeling on the wooden benches, had begun to unwind kilometres of rosary beads in memory of the dead man and beg forgiveness for his soul – obviously ignoring the fact that Teodoro was a good person and that the one sin he had been in the habit of committing, that is, kicking the pathetic excuse for a dog that was currently crouched at their feet, was the only one the two old maids could never forgive him.

Signorina Barbarici was lying in the dark in her room, with a damp cloth on her forehead and her ankles raised, moaning from time to time.

Signor Ciceri had set off for the woods, whistling a happy tune,

42

with his camera over his shoulder, accompanied by the estate manager's youngest son, Cecco, who was pleased to have been granted the privilege of carrying the photographer's tripod and guiding him to the most picturesque spots.

Sitting next to her grandmother, young Cecilia was reading to her in a voice throbbing with emotion:

"'In the days that followed, which loomed before us huge and laden with dangers, grim and solemn and mysterious and unknown, no battles were to be expected, according to the forecasts, but only retreats. Not even two days later . . .'"

The dowager baroness seemed bored.

"'And so we were now prisoners of war, the whole of our platoon. With me—'"

"That's enough, Cecilia, please."

Even when she spoke calmly (which did not happen often), the dowager baroness' words were orders. With ill-concealed chagrin, Cecilia closed the book. "Don't you like it?"

"It's better than the rubbish the Barbarici woman insists on reading to me. But it still makes me sad. I don't need to read stories about a decaying aristocratic family. I just have to look around me."

"Don't say that, Nonna."

"Why on earth not? Did you see the spectacle Lapo made of himself this morning? As drunk as a coachman, and even more vulgar. The only thing the boy's good for is unbuttoning his trousers."

"At least this time we were together as a family. Do you remember when he put out the fire on New Year's Eve?"

The dowager baroness glared at Cecilia.

The previous year, Lapo had been invited together with all the family to dinner at the house of Marquis Odescalchi, the father of Lapo's betrothed, Berenice. The Bonaiuti family had arrived at seven o'clock on the dot, apart from Lapo, who had reached the castle three hours late, in gaiters and crush-hat, and with an alcohol level that had gone through the roof. Having been silently admitted to the dimly lit smoking room by the butler, he had mistaken the function of the sandstone arch towards which he had groped his way (and which was actually a fireplace) and had cheerfully emptied his bladder on the embers beyond the fire screen. The sizzling cloud of steam that rose in consequence of this had scared poor Lapo to death – the rum obviously playing its part, too – and he had run out of the room and across the whole of the dining room at a gallop, with his trousers still unbuttoned, screaming "The devil! The devil!" and blowing on his penis, in full sight of the two families lined up around the table. The engagement had been called off the following day.

Cecilia sustained her grandmother's gaze, and an involuntary smile creased the dowager baroness' lips. Two seconds later, they were both laughing.

❧

"The explanation is simple. He's an invert."

"What?"

Lapo and Gaddo were walking slowly around the pond, Lapo

holding a cup of strong coffee and Gaddo with his hands behind his back.

"An invert. A pederast. If you really want me to be frank, a queer. I suspected as much anyway."

"Lapo, I don't see what that has to do with anything."

"A man interested in cooking, can you imagine? It was obvious from the start that he's a depraved character. I suspected as much, as I said. Last night, as we were waiting for dinner, we had a game of billiards. I told him they had a new batch of girls at Mademoiselle Marguerite's house and asked him if he'd go there with me after dinner as my guest. Do you know what he replied? He told he preferred going to bed with a book. Tell me that's not a queer talking."

"Lapo, sometimes you seem even more stupid than you are. Apart from the fact that, at a rough guess, the man's over seventy..."

"A book, though!"

"He's over seventy, and perhaps . . ."

"And have you seen how he goes dressed? In a top hat and frock coat. I mean to say – a frock coat!"

". . . perhaps some things no longer excite him. That would be understandable. And anyway . . ."

"Things that are thirty years out of date. Only a queer would dress that way, come on."

". . . and anyway I was talking about something else. This fellow entered a room where a dead man was and started sniffing the chamber pot. He was almost dipping those disgusting whiskers of his in it. I could hardly believe it."

"Well, what can you expect of a man who likes sticking it up another man's backside? Anyway, it makes no difference. I don't like this bewhiskered fellow any more than you do, I don't like him one little bit."

~~~

Unaware that the two noble scions disliked him, Pellegrino Artusi had found himself a quiet corner of the garden, behind a cheese-wood hedge, hidden from prying eyes but within earshot in order not to miss the lunch call – lunch would probably be sad but at least it might be substantial.

Artusi had confronted the grim reaper too many times to be disturbed by him. He had been in the war, he had seen his own house looted and his own sisters raped by brigands, he had survived a cholera outbreak that had claimed lives under his own roof. All this he had withstood thanks to his brain, his heart and above all his excellent digestion. So after closing the book, his wandering mind immediately came to rest on the thought of lunch: there might be cholera, typhus, floods and acts of divine wrath, but provided one could have lunch at midday and dinner at seven, the world, as far as Artusi was concerned, was a place where no problems were bad enough to keep you awake at night.

As his thoughts wandered off again, a noise between the leaves attracted his attention. One of the few noises that could shake Artusi and distract him from the thought of lunch: the muffled sound of a girl crying.

~~~

At midday, as expected, the bell rang out across the lawn, informing the whole of the garden that its occupants were expected in the dining room. The residents walked calmly back to the castle. They might not be exactly cheerful, but they were certainly consoled in spirit. Basically, they all needed a touch of normality after the morning's upheaval. Teodoro might be dead, but life goes on and one has to eat, doesn't one?

Being the last to arrive in the dining room, the baron went slowly to his own seat, followed by an austere-looking man with a beard and glasses. Once he had reached the head of the table, he did not sit down, but remained standing in a posture that did not seem his: hands resting on the table, eyes down, the noble arteries on his neck and temples visibly throbbing with vulgar and ill-concealed anger.

After a few seconds, the guests began to look at one another furtively. Then, amid growing embarrassment, the baron turned to the bearded man, who gave a stern, tacit acknowledgement of assent with his eyes.

The baron cleared his throat.

Then he cleared it again.

Then, having caught his breath, he opened his mouth and said in a solemn voice, "I am extremely sorry to have to inform you that we have not gathered here to eat."

Oh, no!

"Dottore Bertini," the baron said, while the bearded man nodded, confirming even to the least attentive that he was indeed the aforementioned Dottore Bertini, "has an extremely regrettable piece of information to share with you. I ask you to listen to him in complete silence."

It was an unnecessary request. There was such tension in the room by now that not a breath could be heard. They all stood there, apart from the dowager baroness (who was paralytic) and Signorina Ugolina Bonaiuti Ferro (who did not understand a damned thing about what was going on around her), and waited.

In the prescribed silence, a chasm opened in Dottore Bertini's beard and a voice much less cavernous than expected, indeed almost like that of a sprite, said, "Thank you, Barone. I must ask you all to be patient for a moment. I have just made a preliminary examination of the body of Teodoro Banti, as a result of which I find myself unable to issue a death certificate."

He looked dead enough to me, Lapo would have liked to have said, but even he realised that now might not be the best time to make jokes.

"In short, ladies and gentlemen," the sprite said from the depths of the woods, "I will need to perform a full autopsy. But even as things stand, I am almost convinced that poor Banti's death was not due to natural causes. To be quite honest . . ."

Here he turned to the baron in evident embarrassment. Without looking at anybody, the baron completed the sentence for him with a kind of furious determination: "To be quite honest, the doctor maintains that Teodoro was poisoned."

Consternation (to say the least).

As the guests remained silent, the doctor continued, "As some of you know, for years now I have been responsible for the health of those living in the castle, at the baron's express request. Consequently, I am familiar with the medical history of every single member of the servant body from birth. Teodoro Banti is no exception."

Having said this, the doctor tilted his head forward onto his chest and seemed to fall asleep, using his beard as a pillow.

After a few moments, Gaddo ventured to open his mouth. "So . . ."

"That is why," the doctor said, as if he had been waiting for that signal to resume speaking, "I was very surprised when Signor Ciceri here present told me that Banti seemed to have died as the result of a heart attack. Because, you see, Banti never in his life manifested any symptoms of heart disease."

This said, he again fell asleep on his beard.

Hearing his judgement called into question, Ciceri made an attempt to speak up. "I hazarded that guess after seeing how flushed his face was . . ."

The doctor woke again. "When I arrived, there was, indeed, intense flushing on the face and neck of the corpse. But not the flushing typical of a heart attack. It was of the pruriginous kind, caused by phlogosis, not by congestion, as witnessed by the scratches on the throat and neck. The poor fellow must have been trying to relieve the dryness of his skin by scratching himself. In addition, the dead man's pupils were dilated in a way that immediately struck me as non-physiological. Last but not least, the position of the body—"

"Are all these grisly details really necessary?" asked the

dowager baroness sternly, breaking in unexpectedly on the doctor's speech.

"These grisly details, as you call them, Baronessa, are the evidence I am putting forward to explain to your noble persons why I cannot issue a death certificate and must, in fact, arrange for the judicial authorities to be notified of what has happened."

"What?" Gaddo said loudly. "Are you intending to bring the police in on this?"

"It is my duty, Signorino Gaddo," the wood sprite said.

"Don't you 'Signorino' me! You were summoned here to certify a death, not to have the police descend on our home!"

"I regret, Signorino Gaddo, that the two things cannot be separated. Just as I have taken an oath to serve the sick, of whatever class, race and condition, so it is my clear duty, whenever a sickness has been inflicted with malicious intent, to report the matter to the authorities."

"Stop acting so high and mighty, you charlatan!" Lapo cut in with his usual tact. "You're nothing but the son of a shepherd, and we paid for your studies so that you could become the quack doctor that you are. Without us, you'd still be rounding up sheep. You should show some respect to those who dragged you from the gutter."

The baron looked at his son as if he had suddenly become phosphorescent.

"With all due respect, Signorino Lapo," the doctor replied with almost complete equanimity, "you paid for my studies, you didn't pay for me. As a human being, I am not for sale. My services may be remunerated, not bought."

"Forgive Lapo," the dowager baroness said. "The poor boy is accustomed to paying for the company of the people he frequents. I hope, Dottore, that you will at least have the decency to spare us all this commotion."

"That, Baronessa, I cannot promise you. Barone . . ."

The baron cleared his throat for the twentieth time. "I have already given orders to my estate manager," he said, "and he has left for Campiglia to collect the local police inspector. If no accidents have befallen them, they will be here shortly."

In other words, farewell lunch.

Saturday afternoon

A real murder. It was almost unbelievable.

Sitting almost contritely, without touching the chair with his back, Ispettore Artistico was taking notes as the doctor's testimony emerged from his beard.

". . . the redness on the face was fading, as I said, but it was quite visible on the neck, which is a typical symptom of belladonna poisoning."

Ispettore Artistico's first reaction when the doctor had sent for him had been one of annoyance. To tell the truth, the doctor had always rubbed him up the wrong way: firstly because he was a socialist, secondly because he was one of the most boring and pedantic people he had ever known, and last but certainly not least, because every time the inspector was out walking with his daughter and met the doctor, the doctor invariably kissed her hand in the most brazenly lecherous manner imaginable. More than once the inspector had been on the verge of cutting short this greeting by thrashing him with his stick. He had even imagined himself scalping the doctor and running off with his beard as a trophy.

"What, however, led me to believe that a poisoning had taken place was the dilation of the pupils, which was quite unnatural.

At this point, I felt the limbs of the corpse with my hands, and obtained an impression of stiffness not compatible with rigor mortis. It was obvious, in other words, that the poor fellow had been prey to convulsions and violent spasms before his death. At this point . . ."

At this point, overjoyed at the fact that he could actually report something that had happened in a nobleman's castle to the police, the doctor had demanded that the authorities be called in. In other words, Ispettore Artistico – who, although continuing to fantasise about the possibility of sprinkling the doctor's beard with pitch, setting fire to it, and savouring the scoundrel's screams of terror, could not help almost liking him at this particular moment. Because for years, Ispettore Artistico had been suffering horribly.

". . . I consider that the poison was in the glass of port wine the poor fellow had in front of him, and of which there still remain a few drops at the bottom. Belladonna actually has a pleasant, sweetish taste, rather like julep, which could easily be mistaken for the sugary taste of that wine. I therefore suggest analysing . . ."

For years – almost ten, to be precise. Since he had been sent to Campiglia Marittima in 1882, after his promotion, the only murder he had had to deal with had been the killing of Ginocchino, the donkey of the baker Artemio, beaten to death with a stick by the tenant farmer Pancacci after the animal had eaten Pancacci's good trousers, which he had hung over a pole in order not to ruin them while he slept off a hangover in the baker's stable. Apart from that, lots of thefts of chickens and a few brawls among peasants who were too drunk to do each other serious harm. What made it worse were the visits at Christmas time by his father-in-law, Lieutenant of Carabinieri Onorato Passalacqua, who had taken part in the expedition which years earlier had put an end to the career of the famous brigand Stefano Pelloni, better known as the Ferryman. Every year without fail, his father-in-law would brass him off with his account of that heroic enterprise, especially the gun battle which had ended with the whole gang in irons and the Ferryman himself mortally wounded – a deed for which the good lieutenant, although not saying it in so many words, implied that he was responsible. And the inspector would sit there, swallowing bile along with Christmas cake, all too aware of the fact that in this godforsaken swamp where he had been sent, even if he was a hero, there would never be a way to show it.

". . . and I'd stake my life on these conclusions. Well, my dear Ispettore, I've done my duty and, believe me, it hasn't been easy. But now I'm happy to leave it all up to you."

"That is my duty, my dear Dottore," the inspector said.

It will be a pleasure, he thought.

"Tell me, Ispettore, what I must do."

❧

The baron sat waiting by the table, upright without being rigid. A true nobleman, in tragedy as in good fortune. The inspector had thought of interviewing him before the others, both as a form of respect and because, at first glance, he seemed the person most affected by the matter.

"A few questions should suffice, Barone. I need to know what happened this morning in detail. A painful duty for you, and, believe me, equally so for me."

In a monotone voice, the baron recounted that morning's events. When he came to the point where he had entered the cellar, the inspector stopped him.

"So the door was bolted from inside?"

"Precisely, Ispettore. In order to enter, it was necessary to force it free of its hinges."

"I understand. Please excuse the interruption. Now, if you'll allow me, I must ask you some specific questions. When you entered, was there a glass of port in front of the dead man, together with the corresponding bottle?"

"Yes, there was."

"Had you ever seen that bottle before?"

"Of course. It's part of my personal reserve. Porto Garrafeira, manufactured by the Niepoort company, and given to me by His Excellency Barone Ramalho, the Portuguese Ambassador, who deigned to visit our vineyards and cellars six years ago."

"So you are accustomed to drinking that wine. When was the last time it was served to you?"

"Last night, after dinner. We gathered in the billiard room to toast the success of my good friend Barone Cesaroni's horse Monte Santo. I had champagne served to my guests, as is fitting for a toast, but I had my port brought expressly for me. You see, I suffer from dyspepsia and cannot indulge in champagne with impunity. So I apologised to my guests and served myself."

"Did you serve yourself personally? I mean, did you pour the port into the glass?"

I'm not a tramp like you, replied the baron's eyes. Since when do members of the nobility do things with their own hands?

"My butler usually caters to my needs, Ispettore, and those of my guests. As I was saying, I had the port poured for me, while the others toasted with champagne. But yesterday I must have been suffering from some indisposition and did not feel at all well, so I barely took a sip of the port."

"I see. How then, Barone, do you explain the fact that the glass found in front of Teodoro was empty?"

The baron gave the inspector a dirty look. After a moment, he smiled slightly. "I've always suspected that Teodoro finished my drinks whenever I left anything. I frequently noticed that he filled my glass once too often, from which I deduced that he was filling it for himself. He was crafty, the poor boy. He knew that I could keep an eye on the level in the bottles, but the glass . . . It was a little trick of his, God rest his soul."

"Excuse me, Barone. You said earlier that in the course of the evening you felt indisposed. Do you mind my asking if you had a bad night?"

"Indeed I did. I didn't get a wink of sleep."

"If I'm not being indiscreet, may I ask what kind of condition kept you awake?"

The baron appeared embarrassed. Some questions are simply not asked, he seemed to say.

"That's quite alright. As I've told you, I often suffer from digestive problems. Because of my stomach ache, my heart was beating faster than usual last night. There were times when I feared I was on the verge of an apoplectic fit."

"I understand. Barone, I see no reason to detain you any longer. I need now to speak to your two sons. I would ask you not to breathe a word to anyone of what we have said, at least until the day is over. My respects, Barone."

"I am most grateful, Ispettore."

❧

One of the most common afflictions of powerful men is to have a stupid son. There is no shortage of historical examples, particularly in politics, from Cromwell onwards: it may be because when you are powerful you have no time to waste keeping an eye on your children, or because if you are influential your offspring are bound to grow up spoilt, but it is not a rare occurrence for a father in a position of authority to be succeeded by an idiot son. As you will all have gathered, Ispettore Artistico had given himself up to such reflections as soon as the baron's younger son, Lapo, had sat down facing him.

Even his way of sitting was irritating: not facing straight ahead, but with the chair angled to the right and his legs crossed, as if instead of dealing with a police officer the young fool were at the café with his friends, and it was in this way, without looking at the inspector, that he had started answering the questions.

"Do you remember at approximately what time the toast finished?"

"I have no idea. I left the company at about eleven in the

evening, and went to the village with some of my companions. I only got back this morning."

"You can confirm, though, can you not, that there was a toast in the course of which you all drank champagne, and only your father was served port?"

"I can confirm that, yes. We hadn't toasted with champagne for a long time. You see, old Cesaroni's horse had won its race, and my father was quite excited."

"I see. Is he great friends with Barone Cesaroni? Or are they partners in the stables?"

"No, not at all. Can you imagine? No, the fact is, my father had bet good money on that horse, which was supposed to be a worn-out old nag and actually won. My father, you know, has always been fond of betting on the horses, and has squandered a fair amount of money on it. A reprehensible vice."

What about you? thought the inspector. The baron's passion for horseflesh was as well known in the area as his son's passion for female flesh (preferably enjoyed doggy-fashion), but the inspector had not expected that it would actually be a member of the same family who would broach the subject.

"I wouldn't have thought, Signorino Lapo, that this was a problem for your father."

"You may think that."

"What do you mean?"

Lapo looked about him circumspectly and put his hands up like someone realising a moment too late that he has just said something he shouldn't. "This is a somewhat delicate matter.

I'm not sure that now is the time to—"

"I am a police officer, Signorino Lapo, not a porter. Delicate matters are my business."

"Of course. The thing is, this is a family affair, and I doubt that it's of any relevance to your investigation. We are entitled to be treated with a modicum of respect, I think."

"Signorino Lapo, let me remind you that I show you respect every time I pretend not to see you commit one of your nocturnal feats. The next time we meet, you may well be directly beneath a street lamp, and it would be hard for me not to recognise you."

Lapo looked down at the floor for a moment, then turned his chair to face the inspector. "Alright, then. A few days ago I was in Mademoiselle Marguerite's house when I overheard something that made my hair stand on end. You know Mademoiselle's house, I assume?"

"I frequently have to make arrests there when the customers start causing a disturbance."

"Then you'll know that the walls are of plasterboard and you can hear every noise from the adjoining rooms. You wouldn't believe the kinds of noises people make in certain situations. Sometimes—"

"Signorino Lapo, I have no interest in these erotic shenanigans. Please get to the point."

"Forgive me. I was merely trying to underline that, however inadvertently, what goes on in the other rooms is common knowledge. Anyway, without wandering off the subject again, no more than a week ago I heard a man talking about my father in the next room, maintaining that he did not pay his debts."

"What?"

"Exactly what I'm telling you. 'All that splendour, and nothing in his pocket,' the man said. 'To keep going he's been forced to turn to moneylenders. Among the guests invited to the castle for the hunt, there'll be one who's there for a very specific purpose.'"

"I see. So you're telling me . . ."

"Precisely, Ispettore. One of my father's guests is a usurer who wants his dirty money back. And I know who it is."

~∗~

Ispettore Artistico walked up and down the room, lost in thought, as he waited to interview the rest of the family.

About what had happened, there seemed little doubt. Someone familiar with the baron's habits had waited for the right moment to poison his drink with a substantial dose of belladonna. The baron, however, probably because he had eaten too much, had barely wet his lips with the port: the indisposition he had described struck the inspector as the typical effect of the ingestion of belladonna. Poor Teodoro, confronted with that almost full glass, had taken it with him to the cellar and drunk it all down, consuming the rest of his days along with the wine.

Lapo's pitiful cock-and-bull story added some further suspicious elements. Obviously, the young layabout had concocted a piece of nonsense off the top of his head to remedy the fact that he had said rather too much, but there was usually no smoke without fire. For the moment, the inspector had decided to play the game:

he would deal with Lapo later. There was something else that needed clarifying now.

Two or three timid knocks at the door transported the inspector back to the reality of the room.

"Come in."

"With your permission," Gaddo said in a steady voice. He was accustomed to it: this was his father's study, and deferentially asking permission to enter was obligatory, not to say natural. Gaddo had never seen anyone enter this study simply by opening the door.

"Please sit down, Signorino Gaddo."

Gaddo did so, taking his place on the chair as if afraid of breaking his bones, and immediately embarking on a series of little movements to adjust the crease in his trousers, his jacket, his watch chain and the chair. He would probably also have changed the position of the table if he had been strong enough. Unfortunately for him, Newton would not allow it: the table was of heavy olivewood, and Gaddo, to judge by his appearance, was the kind of person who would have got out of breath cutting his nails.

The inspector asked Gaddo, as he had asked his father and brother, to describe the events of the previous evening, and Gaddo confirmed what they had said.

"I shan't bother you, Signorino Gaddo, by making you repeat things that I feel I have already verified," the inspector said after two or three questions. "I should, however, like your opinion on the two guests your father invited to the castle for the hunt. Had you met either or both of them before?"

Gaddo lifted an eyebrow. "I don't understand what you're trying to insinuate."

They were clearly off to a bad start.

"As it happens," continued Gaddo, "no, I had never met them, nor did I know them by reputation. I rarely leave the castle. I have everything I need right here. Peace and quiet are essential to my inspiration."

"I understand. And can you tell me anything about the two guests now that you have met them? Do you know, for example, why they were invited?"

Gaddo sighed in a knowing manner. "Signor Fabrizio Ciceri is an expert on photography," he said. "My father summoned him here to photograph our family and the surroundings of the castle. I myself showed Signor Ciceri around the estate yesterday, pointing out some attractive spots and reciting some of my verses composed in those very places, to give him a better idea of the atmosphere."

"I see," said the inspector, who really was beginning to see. Poor Signor Ciceri. "And what of Dottore Artusi?"

"*Signor* Pellegrino Artusi," Gaddo said, emphasising the title, "was summoned here by my father for reasons that are quite unknown to me. It appears my father met him while taking the waters and they struck up a kind of friendship, which I find totally incomprehensible. The man's completely out of place here."

Neither of them speaks well of his father. If they'd been born poor, these two blockheads would probably not even have got out of short trousers, but instead of thanking the Lord who, for reasons known only to Him, provided them with a rich and powerful father, these two happily slander him. Not enough of the strap and too many sweets, that's the problem.

"And why do you consider Signor Artusi so out of place?"

"That should be obvious to you as soon as you meet him. A coarse, jumped-up fellow from Romagna, one of the most vulgar people I have ever seen. He reads books with illustrated covers. And he even writes. Cookery books, can you imagine? How he writes them I don't know, but to judge from the way he pigs himself on his material he must know it like the back of his hand."

~✷~

And now here he was at last, the final resident to be interviewed, Signor (or Dottore) Pellegrino Artusi from Forlimpopoli. His physical appearance, it must be said, somewhat disappointed the inspector, who had been expecting some kind of fiery-eyed gypsy, not an easy-going gentleman with impressive white whiskers who vaguely reminded him of his grandfather Modesto. Be that as it may, this fellow did not leave anyone indifferent. There had not been a single person among those questioned who had not had his say about Artusi. And there had not been two who agreed about why the man had been invited to the castle. Some considered him a usurer, some a sponger, some a kindly old gentleman who had become friends with the baron. The most comical and at the same time most tragic explanation was that provided by Signorina Cosima Bonaiuti Ferro.

The signorina, a classic example of a spinster absolutely with-out attraction, either to the eye or the ear, had told him in a flood of words devoid of both meaning and punctuation that Artusi had clearly been invited by her cousin the baron as her suitor. She had deduced this from the fact that

– she and Artusi had been born in the same year, 1820 to be precise, and when one chooses a companion at an advanced age it is well known that one chooses someone of exactly the same age because that way it is easier to share the infirmities which are such a feature of being old and blah-blah-blah

– Artusi had come from Florence specially and had presented himself in a frock coat, and when one dresses so well it means something because in the countryside people usually go dressed in a less formal manner and blah-blah-blah

– Artusi was neither married nor a widower and she would never have accepted a widower because that kind of thing upset her and men like that who have never married are so few and far between that her cousin the baron must have thought with good reason that Dottore Artusi was a really good catch and blah-blah-blah.

To all this waffle the inspector had lent only half an ear, given that since the beginning of the interview he had found his right leg imprisoned between the paws of the signorina's pet dog, which had begun to mime an unlikely act of sexual congress with his shoe. It is a well-known fact that a dog that tries to make love to your ankle can be quite annoying and a hindrance to concentration, which was why, after a few half-hearted attempts to shake it off gracefully, the inspector had resolved to crush the dumb but troublesome animal between the leg and the foot of the olivewood table with a few well-aimed kicks, while the signorina happily continued her ravings.

Anyway, here was Signor (or Dottore) Artusi. That was the first unresolved question, not a matter of major importance perhaps, but why keep it to oneself?

"Please sit down, Signor Artusi. Pardon, Dottore Artusi."

"Oh, no, please allow me to explain. That's a little misunderstanding that has pursued me for some time. I do indeed frequent the lecture halls of the University, but as a mere interested listener, a curious bystander. I am not entitled to be called Dottore."

A reply given timidly and unemphatically, without any putting on of airs. After which Artusi looked at the inspector as if to make sure he had given the right answer.

Indeed he had. The inspector hated people who pretended to be what they were not, and he knew how much pleasure it gave the son of a shopkeeper to be called Dottore. It was a symbol of revenge, a medal of everyday valour to be displayed to everyone. It was something the inspector knew from personal experience.

Born at Aieta, in the Calabrian hinterland, he had become an Italian together with his region and a doctor of law by studying while still kneading dough. Having started out as the son of a baker, after his graduation and his transfer to Milan he had married the prettiest girl in Maratea, whose parents could not believe they were now related to a graduate and an officer. For him, the word Dottore had meant Open Sesame.

Seeing someone calmly and humbly abjure the title even though he could have usurped it with impunity impressed him.

Artusi was an honest man, and the inspector only liked honest people.

The inspector looked at Artusi and decided to get straight to the point. "Signor Artusi, I have already heard the story of the discovery of poor Teodoro Banti's body several times today. I'm sure you won't mind if, instead of getting you to tell me the same story, I simply ask you to confirm or deny what I have been told thus far."

"Oh, yes, yes, I mean, I am here to be of service. Go ahead and ask."

"Alright, Signor Artusi, can you confirm that the door to the cellar was bolted and that it was necessary to break it down in order to enter?"

"Yes, I can."

"Can you confirm that Banti was on the chair when you entered, and that in front of him was a bottle of port wine and a glass empty but for a dash of the same wine?"

"Indeed I can."

"Can you confirm that, after having entered, you went to the night table situated next to Banti's straw mattress, took out a full chamber pot, and sniffed the said chamber pot for a long time?"

Artusi turned red. "Yes, I did."

"Would you be so kind as to tell me why?"

"Well . . ." muttered Artusi, the flush gradually fading from his cheeks. "The fact is, Ispettore, that when we entered the room I immediately became aware of a characteristic smell, which I did not recognise at first. As we were in the antechamber of a cellar, I thought it was mildew. But . . . you see, in that smell there was a touch of something I knew only too well. I am sure you know, Ispettore, that when a person eats asparagus then subsequently relieves his bladder the urine gives off a somewhat unpleasant odour."

"Of course."

"There you are, Ispettore. The chamber pot inside the night table had exactly that disgusting smell."

"I understand."

"With all due respect, Ispettore, you still lack one necessary piece of information to understand. You see, in the course of the dinner asparagus was served, which is why before going to bed I poured a few drops of turpentine into my own chamber pot to obviate the unpleasantness of which I have just spoken. However, in the course of the afternoon, young Banti had mentioned to me in advance some of the dishes to be served that evening."

"I see. And what of it?"

"Well, Banti told me he could not stand asparagus or courgettes, and would not have eaten them even if forced to do so."

The inspector looked at Artusi with a bovine air.

"You see now what struck me, don't you? We entered a room locked from the inside, in which a particular person often spent time. The said person hates asparagus, and yet his chamber pot had been used lately by someone who had eaten it. I find that a trifle puzzling, if you see what I mean."

Yes, I do. A keen sense of smell, this Signor Artusi. And a quick brain.

"Have you made a study of criminology, Signor Artusi?"

"Oh, no, please. It's just that—"

"Then don't jump to conclusions, Signor Artusi. There may be a thousand explanations. And please do not breathe a word to anyone of what you have told me. Personally, I doubt it is of any importance, but it is best not to speak about it."

"I understand, Ispettore."

"Well, Signor Artusi, for the moment I have nothing else to ask you. Given the late hour, I think it is best to conclude."

"As you wish, Ispettore. I hope I have been of some help."

You have no idea, my dear fellow.

From the diary of Pellegrino Artusi

Saturday, 17 June, 1895

To think that only yesterday, arriving at this manor, I imagined peace and quiet, would be to admit I was an idiot. Today's events have been so numerous, and so absurd, that it seems to me madness to write them all down.

This morning we awoke to a scream and a corpse, which was already a long way from what I consider peace and quiet; as if that were not enough, the dead man did not have the good sense to pass into the other life on his own account, but was reduced to a cadaver by someone else. A police officer (who at least struck me as a decent person) was summoned, and he interviewed all of us and is now, as far as I know, proceeding to question the servants.

But none of this needs to be written about: one writes a diary to jog one's memory, and I shall remember this murder as long as I live, even if I lose the use of my mind. What I prefer to express on these pages are those feelings which my sense of decorum and my advanced age do not allow me to express in the flesh.

Today, having retired to a corner of the garden in search of a little of that peace and quiet I had imagined on arriving here, I was distracted by the noise of a young girl weeping bitterly through the branches; and, looking behind the hedge, I was more than a little surprised to see that it was none other than the proud and beautiful housemaid who showed me to my room yesterday. It is pointless here, with no-one but myself as a witness, to pretend feelings other than those that every man has in seeing a beautiful girl in tears: the desire to take her in his arms and console her, in the various ways that nature suggests, for her sorrows, whatever they may be. Having handed her a cambric handkerchief, I asked her if she had known poor Teodoro well, given that I had noticed she was holding a photographic portrait of the deceased in her hand. After a little more weeping, she told me that she had been betrothed to him, and that they were due to have been married very shortly. Stunned by this, I gazed at the photograph and could find nothing better to say than that he really had been a very handsome young man, thus causing a further outpouring of tears. She told me that the young man had recently found the money they needed to marry, after selling his few possessions to invest in a business together with an acquaintance of his, and he had confided in her that they would be leaving for the city in the following month, and that he intended handing in his notice very soon.

Such a sad story, told by a young woman of such Junoesque features, could not leave me indifferent, and several times during the course of the day I caught myself thinking of what might have been if I were a good deal younger than I in fact am.

By way of contrast, after my interrogation dinner was served. To do justice to this occasion would require the pen of one of those fine French poets so beloved of Signorino Gaddo who derive such pleasure from their own and other people's misfortunes, and who *are so good at narrating the sorrows and anxieties of all and sundry: my own meagre virtues as a scribbler are, I fear, inadequate to the task.*

At dinner, then, I found myself seated between the two Bonaiuti Ferro sisters. The atmosphere was decidedly unreal: one of the two constantly asked me for details of my cooking, the house where I live and my affairs in general, while the other (who it is now clear to me is completely soft in the head) constantly nodded, displaying a three-toothed smile that would have made a pig lose its appetite. This grotesque conversation took place in the most absolute silence, in that none of the other dinner guests had any desire to talk, which is only understandable. To make matters worse, throughout the dinner I had the eyes of the baron's two sons on me, both looking at me as if I had just vomited on my plate.

Of Signorina Cosima's intentions there can be no more doubts, I fear. I got my last two sisters off my hands only with great difficulty, paying a thousand francesconi each out of my own pocket to marry them off, and I have had enough of dealing with old maids about the house to want to have any under my feet again.

I also have a fairly clear idea now of what the baron's two sons think of me; if they could, they would clap me in irons and hand me over to the authorities without further ado, as a usurer and a poisoner.

To sum up, I came here to advise the baron on his kitchens and to spend a quiet week, instead of which I find I am in danger of being either accused of murder or betrothed to a mad old woman who could be silenced only with quicklime. I shall have to follow the story of the two white stones and find a way to get out as soon as possible; after which, if the good Barone di Roccapendente wants to see me again, he will have to wait to be invited to my house.

Sunday morning

On Sunday morning, the castle awoke drenched in rain. The bad weather had begun during the night, and it continued unabated all morning, heedless of the baron's plans (he had been hoping to offer his guests a walk in the woods with rifles on their shoulders, to bag a few fowl to be roasted) and much to the joy of the labourers (for once, they could stay in on a Sunday and wouldn't have to break their backs in the fields). It is particularly awful when it rains and is hot; because staying indoors is stifling, but it is not advisable to go out. Only a madman would go out in such weather. That was why the individual in the oilskin cloak and boots who was heading for the gazebo facing the pond must have been decidedly deranged.

꘏꘎꘏

Having reached the shelter of the gazebo, the madman removed his cloak, revealing two beautiful white whiskers to the world. If the author wanted to show off his pointless erudition, now would be the right moment to tell you that this type of facial appendage is technically called *favoris en côtellette*, and was considered extremely elegant by gentlemen in the mid-nineteenth century. Since, however, the author suspects that very few of you have a genuine interest in the formal classification of the various kinds of whisker, it may be better to drop the matter.

Having also divested himself of his boots, Signor Artusi sat down circumspectly on one of the deckchairs in the gazebo, searched in his jacket, took out the book with the illustrated cover that had so disgusted Signorino Gaddo, and opened it with great pleasure, resting his chin on his chest to be able to read better, and there he remained, like a big walrus with a book in its hand.

One of the problems of having *favoris en côtellette*, as you all know, derives from the fact that, when it rains, they become somewhat wet and, if you happen to have a book in front of you, they tend to drip water on it at the slightest movement. That is probably why, if someone wants to appear really repellent, nowadays, he does not grow side whiskers like an Austro-Hungarian army officer, but gets himself a nice piercing under the lip, which is much quicker.

For this reason, after a few minutes spent dripping over the pages, Artusi closed the book and put it down on the wooden floor of the gazebo. Almost immediately, a cheerful, crystalline voice made itself heard above the rain:

"If you've finished, you could lend it to me."

Artusi lifted his head in surprise, then broke into a genuine smile. "Signorina Cecilia, what a surprise. Please, come and take shelter."

"I thank you, but there's almost no need, it's easing off," said Cecilia, also freeing herself of a kind of rainproof cloak. "Some of the servants told me they had seen you going out, and I thought this was the only place I would find you."

"That was a good deduction. Here I am. Would you permit me to ask you what drove you out into the rain to look for me?"

"You have just done so, therefore it is pointless for you to ask permission. My grandmother wanted you to know that, should you wish to attend Mass, our chaplain will celebrate it in the chapel in the garden at eleven o'clock on the dot. I took the liberty of remarking to my grandmother that you struck me as someone who would be more upset to miss a meal than to miss Mass, and by way of reply here I am."

"I'm sorry, Signorina Cecilia, I shouldn't like anything unfortunate to befall you. As you so rightly observed, I'm not the kind of person to bother with Mass. Please don't misunderstand me: I love the company of priests, but sitting beside me at a wooden table, not standing in front of a marble one."

"Don't worry, I understand you perfectly. As for the walk in the rain, it is an excellent excuse to be alone for a while without anybody asking me what I am doing. I am almost grateful to you. I am surprised, though, that you prefer a creaky wooden gazebo in the rain rather than a comfortable armchair. If I were not afraid of being indiscreet, I should ask you why."

Because that old sow, your aunt Cosima, follows me everywhere I go, Artusi would have liked to reply. This morning at breakfast she pestered me for a good hour, and when I went to get my book I heard that cur of hers barking in the drawing room, which meant that the old woman was there and had probably plumped herself down next to the armchair I had singled out for myself. In addition, the beast was barking undisturbed, without

75

anybody obeying the impulse to give it a kick, a sign that the old busybody must have been on her own. On her own and ready to make eyes at me all morning. I preferred the rain: at least pneumonia kills you quickly.

"A yearning for peace and quiet, like you, signorina," he said aloud. "I am accustomed to an outdoor life, and for years loved walking in the rain. I feel almost rejuvenated when I can still summon up the courage to do so. Alas, that rarely happens these days."

"You mean you used to do it often?" Cecilia sighed. "You must have had quite an adventurous life, Signor Artusi. My father speaks of you as being a man of a thousand talents."

"Oh, your father is too kind."

"I wouldn't say that. You are a successful merchant, you've written a cookery book which I have heard is of great value. And I know you have also written about literature."

"That is correct," said Artusi in a self-important tone. "*Some Observations on Thirty Letters of Giusti*, and a *Biography of Foscolo*. I wrote them, and someone somewhere may even have read them, although I seriously doubt it."

"In any case, you are a person of encyclopaedic culture, and you know how to apply it to a large number of things."

"No, signorina, I am simply someone who has been fooled so many times that he has learned it is better to do things for himself in so far as he can, and trust nothing but his own eyes and his own senses. This is very much the case when it comes to cooking. Anyone can say anything he likes in books, but if once having read my book, the reader is not able to apply my recipe and derive pleasure and nourishment from it, he certainly can't invite me to dinner and have me cook for him. As Giusti says, *Making a book is less than nothing, if the book does not remake people*. And that is the sentence, you know, that gave me the idea of writing my own cookery book."

Artusi looked at the girl, worried that he might be boring her. Seeing that on the contrary the girl seemed curious, he continued, "I have always liked to eat well. Besides, I come from Romagna, where even though we may not be on the level of Bologna, we have a cuisine worthy of respect. Well, living alone as I do, I began to pay a great deal of attention to the food I was eating, and to become interested in the way it was prepared. I read dozens of books and, believe me, they didn't get me very far. Until one fine day, something happened which was the straw that broke the camel's back. I found some fresh lambs' brains in the market, and wanted to fry them in the Milanese way, because when it comes to fried food there is nobody to touch the Milanese. So I took down Luraschi's *New Economical Milanese Cook*, opened it and began."

Looking at his young listener, Artusi assumed an expression of interest turning to dismay, and opened wide his arms.

"I still recall that recipe. It's engraved on my memory. This is what it said" – here he adopted a decent imitation of the Milanese accent – "'Clean and blanch the brain then have it cooked as above: remove it from the brasure, pass it through a sieve, adding a spoonful of flour thickened with two ounces of butyrate, let this fricassee boil for five minutes, stirring it all the while, then add a liaison of two egg yolks, the juice of half a lemon, a little chopped parsley, pour the whole mixture over the brain already cut into pieces, and piece by piece together with a little sauce coat it with breadcrumbs and emborage it, and make it hard by frying in the boiling fat; serve with fried parsley.'"

Cecilia looked at him with a scowl.

"I read it once, and didn't understand a thing," he went on. "I tried again, and thought I had grasped the meaning, and tried to do what I thought I had grasped. I lost my temper and did it all wrong. Those poor brains came out as one of the most disgusting, most inedible fried dishes I have ever come across. I had taken good brains and completely ruined them."

Artusi raised his eyebrows, in that age-old gesture that means, "Would you like to know what I did then?"

"Seeing that delicacy, which had cost me a fair amount of money, reduced to nothing, I was overcome with a fit of anger. Emborage? Brasure? What kinds of words were those? How big was that spoonful meant to be, and how much flour should I have put in? How on earth could I open a book, convinced I would find a recipe in it, and find instead a puzzle to be solved? I thought of what my mother, a woman who could barely write a letter that wasn't full of mistakes, would have been able to put together with that book in front of her, and made my decision."

Artusi stiffened his back, in an almost military fashion, and concluded peremptorily with these words:

"A cookery book should be understandable to all, because we all eat and we all have a right to eat good food well cooked, it should be written in Italian, because we're Italians, and not in that French jargon which is understood only in northern regions, and it should give the quantities, damn it, in grams and litres, which are the same for everyone, and not in ounces or ladlefuls or pinches or hints, when they deign to give the amounts at all. And if such a book does not exist, I'll write it myself. And that's what I did."

Having said this, Artusi looked at Cecilia, with a self-satisfied expression on his face, and smoothed his unkempt whiskers with one finger.

Cecilia laughed. "You see? You are someone who can cope in a thousand situations. In your place, people like my father and my brothers would not have succeeded at anything. And I think that's why my brothers show you their contempt."

"Don't be so hard on your father, Signorina Cecilia. Basically, you have been clothed, educated and brought up by him."

"You're right. Anything I need, I just have to ask for it and it is given to me, provided it is suitable for me. But what I really need – to learn to do something – is either unsuitable or forbidden. So my fate is to remain here, embalmed in all these corsets, waiting for a suitor a little less stupid and unbearable than those who have been presented to me over the past year. So I will get married, have lots of nice children who will grow up just as useless to the world as I am, perhaps even more so, and quite unaware of what is around them and . . . I'm sorry, I'm talking too much."

"I beg you, signorina, continue. It is a pleasure for me to see that at least one of the baron's three children trusts me."

"Oh, as far as that goes . . . Gaddo sees you as someone who has succeeded in doing something, and that irritates him like smoke in the eyes. He isn't stupid, nor is he wicked: if someone taught him, and made him realise that success doesn't descend on one by divine right, just because one is noble, he might succeed at many things."

Cecilia was silent for a moment, as if to convince Artusi that what she was saying was not dictated by affection, but by reality. Given that her interlocutor was silent but looked dubious, she continued:

"The trouble is that my dear brother has no terms of comparison, and this makes him think that he is much more intelligent and cultivated than he really is. He has always found it difficult to make friends, and he grew up together with Lapo, who although he is still my brother is certainly no genius. My grandmother always says of Lapo that the best one can say, if one is forced to say something good about him, is that he dresses well."

Artusi said nothing. Cecilia had not cited herself as a term of comparison, for all too obvious reasons. She was a woman, and this was 1895. At that time, as far as public opinion was concerned, a woman barely had a soul.

This was an era when Italy was taking shape, and people were passionate about politics. They were years in which there was much discussion of unity, constitutions, rights and freedom. Unfortunately, barely two years had passed since New Zealand – a country literally a world apart from us, being on the other side of the globe – had been the first on earth to give votes to women.

As an Italian woman, our Cecilia would have to wait another fifty-one years to vote, assuming she survived cholera outbreaks, two world wars and the three or four pregnancies which presumably awaited her. She could not vote, and she could not be elected. The only possibility she had to play an official public role would be if someone tried to rape her, and failing to do so, killed her: in that case, very probably, she would have been made a saint by popular demand. As a career prospect, it must be admitted that it had its limitations.

All this Artusi and Cecilia said to each other with their eyes, in much less time than it has taken you to read it. After which, Artusi resumed cautiously:

"In any case, signorina, I am pleased that you have honoured me with your trust. Believe me, I am truly touched, and I would be happy to reciprocate."

"Do you mean that?"

"It has been a long time since I last lied to a woman, signorina."

"Good. Then you would be doing me a great favour if you found a way to sprain your ankle."

Ah, it's finally happened, said Artusi's eyebrows. Either I'm becoming deaf, or I'm losing my mind.

"I'm afraid I do not understand."

"You see, Signor Pellegrino Artusi, like you I find the hours spent at Mass could be put to better use. Especially when one finds a person of the world with whom one can converse about things of substance, which is something that rarely happens to me."

"I understand, signorina, but—"

"Please be so good as to let me speak, since you seem to me the only resident of the castle who is kind enough to listen to me when I speak. You are a guest here, and master of your time, which means that you can do what you like, but for me not to be present at Mass would be considered highly reprehensible, and would certainly result in punishment. But, if a guest hurt himself while I was with him, it would be even more reprehensible if I didn't help him. That is why, if you demonstrated that you had sprained your ankle, I would be able to bandage it to perfection, after which we could walk to the castle. You would have to go slowly, since you are infirm, and I, as the master's daughter and an expert nurse, would have to help you. We would miss Mass, it's true, but we would arrive just in time for lunch."

Artusi looked at the girl, and a slow smile wrinkled his stern whiskers.

***

They walked slowly in the sun, Artusi and his makeshift hand-maid, laughing like two old friends or two people amusing themselves behind each other's backs.

They were close to the castle and had slowed down even more. Artusi had already rattled off two or three of his stories, and was now telling Cecilia about the cholera outbreak of 1855, and how he had saved the life of a coachman.

"I had with me this large bag of chamomile, given to me by my father, and I said, 'This poor man is surely in a bad way. Let's try, it won't do any harm.' No sooner said than done. I put a big pan on the fire and made him a chamomile broth, with as much sugar and lemon as I could dissolve in it. Just between ourselves, the thing had a smell so sweet and syrupy that if I had been him, I would rather have given up my soul to the creator than knock that back; but the coachman was so parched by the fever that he drank it all down without leaving a drop. Believe me, because I still have difficulty in believing it myself, the next day the coachman's temperature had gone back to normal and there was not a single symptom left of the cholera. You should have seen him: every time he passed through Florence he insisted on coming and saying hello to me, and he bowed and scraped so much that I was almost embarrassed."

"What a story!" Cecilia sighed as she walked with Artusi holding tight to her arm (quite unnecessarily but, let us be honest about this, he was rather taking advantage). "I envy you, you know, I really envy you. There are few things more beautiful and more honourable than to cure a person and restore him to health, however humble and uncouth he is. I think it gives meaning to a whole life."

"You certainly are good with bandages," said Artusi, and laughed. "Since you bound my ankle, I haven't felt any pain at all."

"Go on, make fun of me. I've read a lot about medicine, you know."

"Really?"

"When I was a little girl, I had the good Canon Mazzi bring me books of all kinds. One day, he brought me *Robinson Crusoe*, and I was fascinated by how a man alone on an island was able to cure himself of his own infirmities with tobacco. I decided to find out more. Every month after that, the canon would bring me a book that he chose from his library, because his predecessor had been very interested in medicine and had put together a fine collection. I could tell you the name of every bone and muscle in your body."

"A genuine passion, then. A very praiseworthy thing."

"For someone else, perhaps. My father found me reading the *Anatomy* of the Salerno School in bed and became furious. Away with all the books I had under my bed and, in order not to fall into temptation, away also with candles for three months. Before going to sleep, if I wanted to take my mind off things, I could say my rosary."

Again, Artusi said nothing.

"I'd give anything to—" said Cecilia, her eyes lowered.

To study medicine, she would probably have said if she had been able to complete the sentence. But that is something we can only imagine. Because just as she uttered the word "to", a shot rang out across the clearing. Followed a moment later by another identical shot.

The two shots filled the space for a moment, and when they faded it was as though something had broken.

Artusi looked at Cecilia, who looked at him in her turn.

By way of reply, a stentorian voice came from the orchard: "Barone! Barone!"

Cecilia turned pale. She looked at Artusi, who looked at her. Then, lifting the hem of her dress, she set off at a run through the mud.

Even though his ankle was fine, Artusi still had a cruise speed equal to two kilometres per hour over dry ground, and had not done any running since 1858. By the time he got to the orchard, a good fifteen minutes had passed since the shots, and the garden was full of people.

Of all of them, the one who stood out was Ispettore Artistico, who was crouching and holding between his fingertips, as if it were a disgusting animal, a hunting rifle with an ornamented stock.

Behind him on the ground, the seventh Barone di Roccapendente lay face down with his legs pulled under him, in a pose that was not at all noble – any more than were the invocations of the name of Our Lord that emerged in strangled cries from his throat – while Cecilia, bending over him, pressed on his bloodstained shoulder.

As Artusi arrived, he was passed by a man on horseback so heavily bearded that it could only be Dottore Bertini. Once he had arrived, the doctor dismounted clumsily and approached the group, crying, "Do you need help? I was here in the hills. I heard shots and screams . . ."

"Yes, we need help," said the estate manager, opening his mouth for the first time that day. "The baron's been shot."

Sunday, lunchtime

The problem with being brought up in a dogmatic way lies in the fact that, if we should ever find ourselves in situations other than the well-known, well-defined ones with which we feel perfectly comfortable, we usually lose our heads.

The rules of etiquette for the respectable nobleman, for example, did not explain at all how to behave when someone shoots our kin through a hedge. It was quite true that this code envisaged a large number of situations in which someone might have the right to shoot someone else, for example in a duel with pistols. If one considered one had been offended in some way, the rules told one everything about the formal aspects of challenging the scoundrel to a duel, and everything one had to do to fire at one's peer according to the rules of good manners. If one behaved properly, following all the dictates point by point – the responsibilities of the seconds, the offer to wipe out the offence, and so on – one could happily riddle someone with bullets without public opinion finding anything to blame one for.

Whereas shooting at someone from behind a hedge was the action of a peasant. It simply was not done. It was a sign of bad manners. The nobleman's code of etiquette did not even deign to consider such an eventuality.

That was why, when the shot had rung out and the baron had slumped to the ground and begun taking the name of the Lord in vain in such an unpleasant manner, the first moment of confusion had been followed by complete pandemonium.

～✖～

Signorino Lapo had turned pale, and when the second shot came, convinced that he was under fire from a sniper, had dived straight into the well.

～✖～

Signorina Barbarici had remained indoors, luckily for her, because otherwise Lapo would probably have landed on her.

～✖～

The dowager Baronessa Speranza, also indoors, was sitting petrified in her wheelchair, looking about in search of her granddaughter Cecilia, the only intermediary between her and the world, seeing that Signorina Barbarici was still in her room.

～✖～

The sisters Cosima and Ugolina Bonaiuti Ferro, hands joined in prayer, were begging forgiveness of Our Lord for their dear cousin's seriously blasphemous expressions, which even when one is lying on the ground with a rosary of bullets in one's back are, as everyone knows, a deadly sin.

～✖～

Signorina Cecilia was outside: having come running, she had bent over her father and, while also invoking divine intervention to strike the two bigoted old maids with a thunderbolt, had torn off his jacket, put a leather glove between his teeth, and was now holding his hand tightly in hers.

❧

Gaddo, after a moment's dismay, had set off at a run after the marksman and had followed his tracks for some thirty metres across the cornfield, after which, worn out from the effort, he had half collapsed and had lain down amid the ears of corn, his heart thumping in his throat.

❧

The dog Briciola had begun barking furiously and had also set off in pursuit of the marksman, probably not so much to make itself look good as because it was aware that with all this commotion there was an increased likelihood of being kicked.

❧

Signor Ciceri had been standing there when the shots rang out, with his magnesium lamp in one hand and his pump in the other, having just taken a photograph of the baron in hunting pose with his two sons, also armed with rifles, beside him, and had not immediately understood what had happened. Now, still standing motionless, he was protecting his precious but extremely fragile bellows camera from the hullaballoo around him and wondering if it was worth the money to put up with all this shambles.

❧

By the time Artusi got to the orchard, then, everything was in a complete mess, so he walked to one side with measured steps and stood observing the scene, puzzling over the fact that whatever untoward incident occurred in and around the castle always seemed to get in the way of lunch. In the meantime, the doctor, having politely but firmly moved Cecilia aside, had bent over her father and given him an injection. Then, having placed a hand over his noble forehead, he had asked him calmly, "I have just given you morphine to help you bear the pain. Now we have to transport you into the house. Do you feel up to moving by yourself?"

The baron did not reply, but his eyes regretted the rules of etiquette he had learned in his youth, which prevented him from telling another person to go to hell in public. After a moment, he shook his head.

"I thought so. Your servants will prepare a stretcher. Until we get you to the house, you must absolutely avoid moving. I don't want earth or other dirt to come in contact with the wounds." The doctor turned to Cecilia. "Did you keep your father still, in a prone position, and put a glove in his mouth?"

Cecilia nodded.

"Well done, signorina. You did what you had to do and what you could do, no more and no less."

⤚⤙⤚

While the wounded man was loaded onto a plank of wood and carried home, the doctor approached the inspector and knelt next to the rifle.

"What does this thing shoot? Could I see the cartridge?"

Without saying a word, the inspector opened the breech and took out one half-scorched cylinder and another that was almost intact, which he opened with a small knife. "Large bullets, for shooting boar. Quite crude."

"Luckily for us."

The inspector gave the doctor a dirty look.

"The greatest danger is infection. If they had been small pellets, fragments of shirt would have gone everywhere in the wound, and the cotton would have rotted and caused serious problems. With large bullets I will have bigger pieces to take out, which should be a lot easier."

"I could help, if you wish," said Artusi calmly. "I've been following Professor Mantegazza's anatomy and physiology lessons for years now, and I could be of some use, but only if you think so, of course."

The doctor looked him up and down for a moment. He was about to reply that he would prefer to operate alone when an echoing voice roared, "What's all this about help? Arrest him! Arrest that scum from Romagna!"

The three men turned, and did not see anyone.

"It was he! He wasn't with us when the shots were fired, nor did he come to Mass! He's a scoundrel, a usurer and a rogue! Arrest him immediately, for heaven's sake!"

The inspector looked around, then understood. With a resolute step, he walked towards the well.

"Signorino Lapo, is that you?"

"Who the hell do you think it is, the old paralytic? Arrest that scoundrel and get me out of here. But first arrest him, damn it!"

"Signorino Lapo," said Artusi, "I'm sorry to disappoint you, but at the time the shots were fired, I was with your sister Cecilia some considerable distance from here. I could not have shot your father unless I had used a cannon, which I am not in the habit of taking with me when I go for a walk."

"How dare you, you bastard? We give you our hospitality and you . . . Ispettore, don't you understand? Arrest him!"

"Excuse me, Signorino Lapo, I am not accustomed to taking orders from anyone below me," the inspector yelled down into the well in a harsh but amused tone. "Anyway, the important thing is to make sure you are alright. We're going to pull you out now. Are you injured?"

"I hit my head," said Lapo after a moment, in a shaky voice.

"Don't worry," said the inspector. "The doctor will take care of your father now, and later, when you've been taken out, he'll see to your cranium." Under his breath he added, "Not that it can be any worse than it already was . . ."

~✦~

Signorino Lapo was pulled out of the well and also stretchered to the house on a plank of wood. The doctor, Cecilia and the servants had all gone now, and only the inspector, Artusi and Signor Ciceri remained in the orchard. After a few minutes, Gaddo reappeared, sweating profusely and red in the face. He approached the inspector, bent down with his hands on his knees, and began taking long deep breaths.

"Did you see who it was?" asked the inspector.

"They ran faster than me," said Gaddo, shaking his head. This was not of much help, given that the only person it ruled out was the dowager baroness. After a few more breaths, though, Gaddo resumed, "Of one thing I am sure. They had long hair, a long dress and broad hips. It was a woman."

"A woman?" said the inspector.

"I'm certain of it. I didn't see her face, and I'm not an expert like my brother, but I can tell the difference between a man and a woman, I assure you."

"If you'll allow me," said Signor Ciceri, "I, too, as I was taking the photograph, had the sense that something was moving behind the hedge. And I had the distinct impression it was a young woman."

"What? Would you mind repeating that?"

"I'm sorry, Ispettore, I am sure of what I said. I—"

"No, forgive me. You were taking a photograph when the baron was shot?"

Signor Ciceri nodded, a little disconcerted at first, then raised his eyebrows knowingly.

"How long does it take to develop a photographic plate?"

"It's an albumin plate . . . I must take it to my darkroom, expose it to light and then fix it. A few hours at the most."

"Good. May I ask you to begin immediately?"

"As you wish, Ispettore."

The man's a nasty piece of work, but sometimes you need people like him.

꧁꧂

Walking up and down the baron's study, Ispettore Artistico was thinking fast.

A woman.

A woman who could have slipped into the cellar on Friday

evening to poison the bottle – poison being a typically female weapon. A woman who was then unwittingly trapped in the room when Teodoro bolted the door and knocked back the poisoned drink intended for the baron. And who was not seen by anyone in the morning simply because she had hidden somewhere in order not to be seen by the butler. She had had to spend the whole night in the cellar without attempting to open the door. Not that it would have been easy to open the door in the dark. Teodoro might have been awakened by the noise. What she had not realised, of course, was that the poor butler was no longer in a position to wake up.

In the morning, when the body was discovered, since nobody thought there had been a murder nobody had bothered to search the cellar. In the confusion that followed, it had been easy for her to slip out and mingle with the others.

However, anyone spending a night locked in a room will have to have a pee sooner or later. It just isn't possible to hold it in all night. A man might, but certainly not a woman. And that explained the smell of asparagus.

The other result of spending the night in a damp cellar carved out of volcanic rock, heavy with saltpetre, at a temperature of seven or eight degrees, would be to catch a cold. Had there by any chance been someone the next day who had red eyes and a runny nose?

Of course there had. That beautiful blonde housemaid with the ice-cold eyes and the arse that could have been painted by Botticelli.

A knock at the door. Come in, Parisina. The great cook, the pride of the house. If I've understood correctly, the one person here who knows everything about everybody is you. So now it's my turn to cook you a little.

Short and fat but compact rather than obese, she must have been plump and pretty when she was young, with the kind of figure that is no longer in fashion today but can still strike sparks beneath the sheets. Now, in spite of arms as big as meat loaves, there remained something of the old grace: in the way she held her head, with her chin high and her eyes darting in all directions, which clashed somewhat with her big apron and flour-covered hands.

"Sit down, Parisina. I just have to ask you a few questions."

"You already asked me a few questions last night."

Why are people who cook well always as friendly as a fork in the eye?

"I know, Parisina, but now I have to ask you a few more, given that somebody shot the baron not long ago, as I'm sure you know."

"All I know is that for two days running I've had to throw lunch away. I made boar with plums for the gentleman with the whiskers, who says he knows about food, and now I have to throw everything away, because that's a dish you either eat hot, as soon as it's made, or it starts to smell like a pigsty and becomes as heavy as an iron."

"Boar with plums?"

Parisina looked at the inspector. There was no need to say anything more.

"So, how was it?"

"My God, Parisina," said the inspector, polishing off the plateful of boar she had put in front of him ten minutes earlier, "it was divine. Good enough to lick your moustache. Now, let's get back to us. Did you hear that it was apparently a woman who shot the baron?"

"A woman? What am I supposed to say to that, Ispettore? There are plenty of women here among the servants. But the maids don't know how to shoot, believe me."

"I didn't say it was someone who knows how to shoot, Parisina. As it happens, whoever it was missed the baron from a distance of four or five metres. Someone who knew how to shoot wouldn't have missed like that, believe me."

"I don't know. That may be so."

"Now what I wanted to ask you is if you remember who was there when you gave Signorina Barbarici first aid yesterday."

"Of course I remember. Made a lot of fuss about nothing, that one."

It is obvious that strong emotions help us to remember things precisely, as those who know about mnemonics maintain. It does not matter if these emotions are extremely painful or incredibly satisfying. Any man can remember where he was when he was dumped for the first time by a girlfriend, just as many of us could describe in detail the funeral of our own mother-in-law.

In the same way, Parisina began to rattle off a list of names to the inspector, most of which he did not know. Agatina was not among them, even though he remembered her perfectly (see above).

"I see. So the only person who wasn't there was Agatina the housemaid."

"No, Agatina wasn't . . ." She broke off. "Ispettore, don't even think about it."

"Pardon me, but what exactly am I not supposed to think about?"

"Don't play the fool, Ispettore. First you tell me it was a woman who shot the baron. Now you're asking me if Agatina was there when we found poor Teo dead in the cellar. Why all this interest in Agatina?"

"I get the feeling you understand perfectly well. The person who shot the baron and then ran off through the cornfield was seen from behind. It was a woman. A woman with blonde hair."

"Oh, I can just imagine Agatina running in her condition!"

"Forgive me, but what condition is that?"

"No, I mean . . . with that maid's dress all the way down to her feet, and those little shoes . . ."

The inspector lifted his gaze from the cook's mouth and looked her straight in the eyes. "As a cook, I am sure you are exceptional, Parisina. As a liar, you leave a lot to be desired."

The cook said nothing, merely looked angrily at the inspector. Next time I serve you boar it'll be poisoned, said Parisina's expression.

"In what condition is Agatina?"

"What condition do you suppose she's in, the poor thing? She's pregnant."

Bull's eye, thought the inspector.

"Do you have any idea who the father is?"

"Agatina was engaged to—"

"I didn't ask who she was planning to walk down the aisle with. I asked if you know who usually slept with Agatina."

"How on earth should I know? Good Lord, I stay in the kitchen, cutting, skinning and gutting, and pretty much minding my own business. This is a castle, Ispettore, full of nobles and servants. And ever since the world began, the nobles stand up straight and the servants bend. Agatina, though, is a bit stiff and doesn't bend easily. Ask Signorino Lapo, he knows what I mean. Last year he tried to get her in a corner, and she gave him a blow with her knee below the belt that he still remembers. If his testicles were meatballs before, she turned them into pork chops. And you know what—"

At that moment, there was a knock at the door, and Parisina fell silent.

"Who is it?" barked the inspector.

"It is I, Ispettore. Fabrizio Ciceri. I have the developed plate with me."

"Come in. Parisina, I must ask you to leave us alone. Go back to the kitchen."

"Oh, yes, I'm going back to the kitchen. And don't worry, I'm not coming out again."

As the cook left the room with all the dignity of which she was capable, Signor Ciceri approached the inspector with a conspiratorial air. In his hand, he held a black box.

Without saying a word, he solemnly placed the box on the table and slowly lifted the flat lid, as if afraid to startle the image with the sudden light.

The photograph was quite sharp. In close up, the baron in an upright pose, with his chin up and a rifle slung over his shoulder, his eyes keen and alert. Next to him, Lapo in a shooting jacket and a ridiculous but fashionable plumed hat, also carrying a rifle, and Gaddo leaning on his rifle, the stock of which rested on the ground, and looking the least threatening of the three.

Behind them, a girl with light-coloured hair could be seen through the hedge, holding a double-barrelled firearm.

If it was not Agatina, it was her twin sister.

Sunday, teatime, more or less

Ispettore Artistico was on fire.

On the one hand, he was certain who had shot the baron, and therefore who had unwittingly killed poor Teodoro instead of poisoning the designated victim.

On the other hand, this certainty was not enough. After all, once you have correctly identified the illness afflicting your patient as appendicitis, you can't just fold your arms and hope the fellow will cure himself because you have told him exactly what he has. If you don't operate on him, he'll kick the bucket all the same.

So, before the inspector could get too overjoyed, he still had to catch Agatina. In order to help him do so, he had summoned to the castle the only two men he had at his disposal, Chosen Officer Asmodeo Bacci (chosen by whom and to do what, God alone knew) and Regular Officer Ivo Ferretti, and set them the task of scouring the countryside in search of the fugitive.

As he walked quickly across country, trying to spot the black dress and golden hair of the housemaid with the itchy trigger finger, the inspector saw fragments of his future life passing in front of his eyes.

Invitations from the baron to dine at the castle of Roccapendente for the man who had saved his life and the lives of his family.

Christmases when his father-in-law's stale, overblown story, which rose every year like the dough for the panettone, would be put in the shade by the hunt for the beautiful markswoman, and the photograph (of which the inspector would demand a copy) showing the Junoesque poisoner getting ready to bring her mission to its conclusion would pass from hand to hand, while the inspector smiled knowingly, and his father-in-law—

A gunshot interrupted the inspector's mental Christmas, and he turned.

From the top of a hill, Officer Bacci was waving his rifle and yelling.

The inspector set off at a run.

Coming within ten metres of the officer, he cried, "Did you get her?"

By way of reply, Bacci approached the inspector and pointed to the plain below them, where a black-clad figure was running across a field of sunflowers. Behind, some twenty metres away, Ferretti was following it at a growing distance, given that Ferretti was about fifty years of age and weighed some hundred kilos and cross-country running was not exactly his speciality.

"Ferretti will catch her now."

The inspector cursed silently. Reaching Bacci, he snatched the rifle from his hands. "And what are you doing here?"

"I'm keeping the situation under control."

The inspector raised his eyes to heaven, which he held responsible for landing him with someone like Bacci. "Listen to me carefully, you blockhead," he said without even looking at him. "You and I are going to run after that woman. You don't need your rifle, it would only weigh you down. If you stop even for a moment, I'll stop, too. But after I stop I'll take aim and shoot you. Got that?"

༚ৡৡৢ

In the castle, the few residents not directly involved in what had happened were waiting for news of the wounded man. The atmosphere was so laden with tension that not even Signorina Bonaiuti Ferro uttered a word. At last, preceded by the shuffling of feet, Dottore Bertini came in, followed by Cecilia. Given the thickness of the doctor's glasses and the luxuriance of the vegetation on his face, it was impossible to tell how the wounded man was from his expression. Turning his myopic gaze around the room, he spotted the dowager baroness and turned to her.

"Baronessa . . . "

"I know I'm Baronessa, Dottore," said old Speranza, the harshness of her voice just a little cracked with tension. "Please get to the point."

"The baron has a number of wounds to his shoulder and neck, caused by the bullets. None of them have affected any vital organs. I extracted from the wounds various fragments of shirt, which all match the holes left in the garment by the bullets. There should be no more extraneous fabric left in the wound. I then proceeded—"

"Dottore, nobody here doubts your competence. Forgive us, but we do not want a description. What we want is to know how my son is."

"Your son is well. He will have to rest for a few days, and keep his arm still, but he is not in any mortal danger."

The room heaved a sigh of relief.

~❧~

It was not easy to catch Agatina. Nor was it especially glorious. In the end, Bacci, having been well motivated by the inspector, managed to throw himself on her just as she was about to jump down from a scar into a little grove of acacias. By the time the inspector arrived, the girl had already been handcuffed and Officer Ferretti had sat down on her, with obvious satisfaction. Without saying a word, the inspector clasped his hands together.

It was over.

~❧~

The doctor's announcement was followed by a moment of euphoria. The dowager baroness had given orders to the servants to bring tea with fruit tarts, and everyone had stood up and was now chatting. The arrival of the tea and the carbohydrates further contributed towards enlivening the room. Apart from anything else, the denizens of the castle had skipped lunch for two days in a row and it is a well-known fact that when the stomach opens up after a period of being tight with tension, it needs to be satisfied.

Artusi had just polished off his third tart when Signorina Cosima crept up behind him.

"Signor Artusi, have you seen what wonderful tarts our Parisina makes?"

Artusi nodded and tried to say something, but was overtaken by her.

"They hardly need chewing, they melt so in the mouth, not like the sweets at Ussero's café in the village, the one with the silvered windows, although he does make a tiramisù you must taste, but not now in summer because mascarpone is heavy in summer, as you know, and if you eat it then the same thing may happen to you that happened to the poor bishop two years ago when he drank hot chocolate on the twelfth of August and then took part in the procession carrying the Holy Sacrament, and well, what with the weight and the chocolate he had a natural disaster and also had to be carried in the procession, the poor man, you could smell him from a long way away . . ."

While the signorina prattled on, Artusi had remained motionless, without even removing the tart crumbs from his whiskers. All around, the others were happily chatting away, without offering him the slightest bit of help. He tried two or three times to open his mouth, but immediately resigned himself. After what seemed an infinite length of time, the signorina mounted a direct attack.

"Do you like Japanese carp, Signor Artusi?"

"I'm afraid I've never tasted it, signorina."

"No, no, what are you saying? My cousin the baron has an ornamental pond not far from here, and a short while ago some Japanese carp were put in it, kai they are called, they're very colourful and really beautiful to look at. If you've never seen them, would you like to go with me to the pond? They are really exceptional fish, you will see, and I can even tell you the habits of some of them. For example, there's one of them that—"

"Cosima," said the dowager baroness with the resignation of

someone explaining things to the mentally deficient, "a hunt for a murderess is in progress outside. We even heard shooting some time ago. I don't think it would be such a good idea to get in the way of the chase and expose our guest to the risk of being shot. Signor Artusi, don't you agree that now may not be the opportune moment?"

"Indeed, Baronessa, I fear you are absolutely right. Signorina Cosima, I'm sorry, but I believe it may be necessary to postpone this pleasant excursion."

Artusi looked at the baroness for a moment. No, it was just a fleeting impression. Elderly baronesses do not wink.

❧

"So you won't be making the acquaintance of the Japanese carp today. All to the good, trust me. I have the impression you would have found them somewhat inedible."

"Please don't joke, Signorina Cecilia."

"Who's joking? The last man my aunt Cosima took to see the carp, Signor Giacinto Fioroni, left that very evening, claiming that his brother, the commander, was dying and had telegraphed asking to see him. The visit must have done him good, because my brother Lapo saw old Commander Fioroni two days later, I leave you to guess where."

As she spoke, Cecilia avoided looking at Artusi: she felt too much like laughing. And it was not possible to laugh today, it would not have been appropriate.

"Anyway, as soon as Agatina is captured, I'd advise you to tread carefully."

"Speaking of which, signorina, I must thank you. Now that the burden of suspicion has been lifted, I must tell you how grateful I am to you for having shown me your trust. It was of great comfort to me. Just as, it must be said, Signor Ciceri's passion for photography was of great help to the police."

"Yes, you're right."

Hold on, Pellegrino. There's something going on here.

One of Pellegrino Artusi's main gifts was his ability to read people's expressions and gestures, a natural talent which he had refined in his long years spent selling silk to half of Tuscany. To observe the customer moment by moment as you speak to him, to see his reactions: unlike the mouth, the body never lies. Eyes that narrow, arms that are folded, feet that point in a different direction from you, and all the other clues that you need to fear, because they indicate that the customer is unhappy, distrustful, bored.

When Artusi had mentioned Signor Ciceri, Cecilia had folded her arms and clenched her fists, simultaneously turning a few degrees towards Artusi – and, as he immediately verified, in such a way as to point her feet away from Signor Ciceri.

Anger, contempt and fear.

After which, she had lowered her eyes and begun carefully removing imaginary crumbs from her dress.

For reasons known only to me, I don't like what I've just heard, screamed Cecilia's behaviour.

"Signorina..."

"Go on."

"May I ask you if you have a problem with Signor Ciceri?"

"A problem? No, not at all."

Now it was the turn of imaginary hairs to be removed from her dress.

"Signorina, permit me to be frank, since it seems to me that frankness is something you appreciate. Your own honesty and lack of guile make it impossible for you to conceal feelings of approval or disapproval. I am somewhat older than you, signorina, and I owe my wealth and indeed my life to the fact that I am not easy to deceive. Having said that, I have no wish to force you to tell me anything, but only to let you know that if there is some way in which I can be of help to you, it would be an honour and a duty for me to do so."

Cecilia straightened her back and smiled. "Forgive me, Signor Pellegrino. It was not my intention to deceive you. There is a specific reason why I trust and respect you. For the same reason I do not trust Signor Ciceri at all."

"On this, signorina, we harbour similar feelings."

"They are not merely feelings, Signor Pellegrino. I don't know if I should tell you this."

"I cannot oblige you to do anything, signorina. You must judge for yourself."

"Then let's do it this way," said Cecilia looking at Artusi with a conspiratorial air. "I will tell you the reason if you explain to me what *tommasei* are."

For a moment, Artusi was stunned. Then the clue, having gone through his brain, was transformed into an explanation and reached his eyes. Which opened wide.

Now he's going to kill me, thought Cecilia.

After half a second, Artusi broke into a smile that lifted his whiskers, and looked at Cecilia with surprised amusement.

Clever girl. What initiative.

"I had to see who I could trust," continued Cecilia. "Of my family, of course, I was certain. Of the guests, one never knows. The world is full of wicked people. The surest way I could think of was to see if you kept a diary, and, having found it, to read it."

"I see. And I imagine you found Signor Ciceri's diary, too."

"Not exactly, Signor Pellegrino."

"What, then?"

Cecilia told him.

~❧~

By the time Ispettore Artistico reached the castle, the news had already arrived. That was why the moment he appeared in the doorway of the drawing room, even though somewhat muddy and unpresentable from his cross-country run, he was greeted by spontaneous applause.

Amid smiles, handshakes and pats on the back, the inspector received various offers of tea and tart, which he gratefully accepted. But those who yearned for a thrilling account of the chase across the fields were destined to be disappointed.

"I am sorry, ladies and gentlemen," he said as soon as he had swallowed his last enormous bite of fruit tart, "but at the moment my first wish is to make sure of the condition of the two casualties. Once I have done that, and carried out certain formalities, we will be able to speak."

"We want at least to know that you will stay for dinner, my dear inspector," said Baronessa Speranza with dignity. "I am stuck here in my wheelchair, so you won't deny me the right to a little adventure, even if only at second hand."

"I shouldn't like to be too much trouble . . ."

"It's no trouble at all. Please be reasonable. My son owes you his life, and here you are talking about trouble. I shall have the cook informed immediately."

"Baronessa, I am honoured. Now could I pay a visit to the two patients?"

❧

It was not so much out of Christian charity or any hankering to be a Red Cross nurse that the inspector wanted to see the baron and his extremely spoilt son as to satisfy his curiosity on a number of points. Or rather, to gain a clearer understanding of what had happened.

Where he came from, it was not unusual for one of the members of a band of cutthroats to shoot the leader. Usually that happened because the brigand in question wanted to become the new leader, and the torch was not passed from one thief to another by holding a board meeting and passing a vote of no confidence in the managing director, as happens nowadays. Therefore, there was always a valid motive to shoot someone within one's own band.

But what possible motive could a housemaid have to shoot a baron? She could hardly proclaim herself baroness. There had to be a reason to attempt to murder someone: jealousy, self-interest, revenge; you certainly didn't shoot your own master without a motive. *Ergo*, before bringing the guilty party to trial, the inspector needed to see things clearly.

～✱～

"How are you feeling, Signorino Lapo?"

"Not at all well, believe me. My head has been aching all day, and if I try to get up I am overcome with dizziness. Have you arrested him?"

"Yes, Signorino Lapo, we have arrested the culprit. And it's not a him, it's a her. Your housemaid, Agatina."

"What? Agatina?"

"Haven't they told you anything?"

"No, I dozed off after they brought me here. The doctor must have given me something to make me sleep . . . But how can you be sure it was Agatina?"

"She was seen, Signorino Lapo. And photographed by Signor Ciceri, in the act of firing. A real stroke of luck."

"Agatina . . . Incredible. Although the girl does have a certain inclination to violence, I think."

"Really? Do you know that from experience?"

"No, of course not. It's just an impression. And so you say the usurer had nothing to do with it?"

"Signorino Lapo, whatever gave you the idea that Signor Artusi is a usurer?"

"Good Lord, Ispettore. I told you the other day—"

"The other day you told me a heap of nonsense. I did not pick you up on it only because I had promised myself to return to the subject later. So, do you want to tell me why you have reason to believe that your father borrowed money from a usurer?"

"What are you talking about? My head really hurts. Would you mind—"

"Signorino Lapo, I have no intention of moving from here until you have told me how you found out about these things."

Lapo sighed, then, pulling himself up onto his two elbows, he pointed the inspector in the direction of a writing desk. "Open that drawer."

The inspector did as he was told.

"Inside, under the smoking things, there is a letter on unheaded paper. I found it among my father's things two days ago. Take it, read it, and then go to hell."

"Good evening to you too, Signorino Lapo."

❦

"May I come in?"

Entering the room, the inspector saw the baron lying in bed, his back raised on several pillows. The room smelt of alcohol and sickness. As he closed the door behind him, Artistico had the impression that the baron was more or less asleep. Probably the effect of morphine, and the sudden reduction of excitement following all these events – after all, it doesn't happen every day that people shoot at you, unless you are at the front. Better this way, the inspector thought. If he's a little dazed, he won't show so much resistance. Of course, clothes and demeanour count for a lot. Lying in bed with a cloth on his forehead, breathing in a laboured fashion, he did not seem so much like a baron. Obviously, a noble title did not protect one from the consequences of bullets.

"Oh, Ispettore." The baron opened his eyes, squinting to see better. "Come in, come in. It's a pleasure to see you."

"Thank you, Barone."

Let's see if you still think that way in half an hour.

"I heard a big commotion and even some applause coming from the drawing room," said the baron, trying with some difficulty to sit up. "Did what I think happened actually happen?"

"Indeed it did, Barone. We have captured and arrested the person who shot you."

At this point, it seemed to the inspector, the baron should have asked who could possibly have dared take him as a target, or some such magniloquent expression. Not a bit of it. The baron panted briefly, then said weakly, "My congratulations. You have done well. Better than well, superbly."

"Aren't you curious to know who it was?"

The baron looked at the inspector as if only now becoming aware of his presence, and after clearing his throat a few times said, "I am somewhat afraid to ask."

"Afraid?"

"Afraid, fearful, terrified, call it what the devil you like," said the baron, gradually regaining his command of speech as well as his nobility of appearance. "This morning I was shot in the back, and now you are about to tell me that a guest of mine, or one of my servants, had no qualms about trying to kill me, and more than once. Yesterday, when you spoke to me, I confess I could hardly believe you. I was convinced that you and the doctor were mistaken, or perhaps I was confusing my hopes with my beliefs. Now . . ."

"I'm sorry, Barone."

I did warn you, my friend. You could have been a little careful before handing out all those rifles.

"Go on, then, Ispettore. Who was it?"

"Agatina."

"Who?"

"Agatina, Barone. Your housemaid."

"Agatina?" The baron seemed dumbfounded. "But she doesn't even know how to shoot . . ."

"Luckily for you, Barone. Being a woman, and untrained in the use of firearms, she could not know what happens when one shoots. The recoil probably deflected the trajectory of the bullets."

"Agatina. I can't believe it."

"Nor can I, Barone. Or rather, I do believe it, because I saw her with my own eyes. The trouble is, I can't explain it. That's why I'm here."

"I don't think I quite follow."

"Barone, nobody shoots people without a motive."

"And why should you care about the motive? Isn't it enough that someone shot me in the back?"

"No, Barone, it isn't. I'd like to—"

"You'd like. I opened my doors to you, I let you conduct your investigations even though I had guests, and I bore your questions and your meddling. And now, after telling me that you have found and arrested the person who shot me, you . . . What's that you're holding?"

"A letter, Barone. But before showing you the contents, I should like to ask you a question."

That's all I needed, said the baron's eyes. Ask it quickly and then get out of my noble sight.

"I have to ask you, Barone, about the current state of your finances."

The baron looked at the inspector stupidly. "Would you mind repeating that?"

"I asked you, Barone, in what situation your income is at the moment."

"How dare you? I do not tolerate such questions in my house! I have been assaulted, attacked, and you come here and ask me if I am rich. Everybody knows I am rich! Look around you, and then tell me if a pauper could afford all this. Have you understood, you damned—"

"Careful, Barone. Don't even think of finishing that sentence with the word 'Southerner.'"

"Or what? What would you do? Who the devil do you think you are? I . . ."

The baron tried to rein in the very plebeian fit of rage that had overwhelmed him. He fell back for a moment on the pillows, then pulled himself up again on one elbow.

"This is my home, Ispettore. My name has been law on these lands for more than three centuries."

"I understand, Barone. Although it might be more accurate to say 'was law'. I must point out that we are no longer in your private fiefdom, Barone, we are in Italy. You no longer have the power of life and death over your tenants, and you no longer make the rules. Your name entitles you to a place in history, not to privileges."

If the baron had been in full health, the conversation would certainly not have ended there. However, the fact that one of the two interlocutors had been riddled with bullets a few hours earlier, and therefore was not at the height of his strength, decided the matter in practical terms. As so often, the fact that the inspector's arguments were objectively stronger had made no difference to the debate.

While the baron was recovering from the effort he had made, the inspector opened the envelope and took out a letter which he handed to the baron. On the letter, in shaky handwriting, was the following message:

Florence, 10 June, 1895

My dear Barone,
I am writing to remind you that two months ago, on 10 April of the current year, I lent you the sum of ten thousand lire in cash after you had revealed to me that you needed money to conclude certain business affairs in the city.
Having asked twice and with the greatest courtesy, and not having received any reply, I now find myself in the position of having to ask you to settle your debt in person.
Certain of your understanding,

The signature was an illegible scrawl.

❧

"Where did you find this letter?"

"It was given to me by your son Lapo."

The baron said nothing, but the way in which he looked at the inspector was sufficient. If I had gone to the brothel that day, said those eyes, I would have spared myself a mountain of troubles in the days to come.

"Annoyed because you always refused his requests for money, your son searched in your drawers to see what he could filch, but what he found was this. From it he deduced that one of the two guests due to come here for the weekend was the author of the letter."

"That son of mine . . ." said the baron with a sigh. "When it comes to money, then he knows how to use his head. Alright, what do you want me to say? I've had a few bad years recently. I admit I borrowed money."

"Was that why you toasted your victory on Friday? You had just won the sum that allowed you to settle your debts before there were serious consequences."

"Exactly," said the baron very softly, almost imperceptibly. "Now would you be so kind as to leave me in peace?"

"First, Barone, I need to ask you one more question."

"Alright. Go on."

The inspector took a deep breath.

❧

"You're mad."

"We're not talking about me, Barone. Please answer the question."

"But good heavens, man, do you really believe—?"

"Barone, I asked you a question."

"No, no, no and once again no!" A brief pause to violate the Second Commandment, about which there is no need to write in detail.

"Barone—"

"Barone my arse! Stop reminding me of my title every few seconds, seeing that you don't show me the slightest respect. I will tell you this once and once only: I have never had carnal relations with that housemaid. Never. I didn't even know she was pregnant. I can't be the father of any child that creature is carrying in her womb, and I don't even care for her. Now get out of my sight and out of my house, otherwise I'll have you thrown off the top of the hill, whether this is Italy or the Grand Duchy or whatever."

Sunday, at dinner

On Sunday evening, dinner was served in the Olympus room, as always, but the analogies with the previous evenings, it must be said, ended there.

～※～

In the first place, the master of the house was not present. The baron had in fact remained in his room, partly because he was still feverish from his wounds and partly because he had been told that his mother had invited the inspector to remain for dinner and it was impossible to withdraw an invitation, let alone go against one's own mother. So the baron had remained in his room and was not eating. This evening he was not even hungry.

～※～

The one eating slowly and circumspectly was Lapo, who in spite of the serious injury to his head (actually a mere graze, but as well as being spoilt and vain this noble scion was also a bit of a cry-baby) had presented himself at dinner looking as spruce as he could.

～※～

The one eating with renewed gusto was Signorina Barbarici, who was quite back to normal now that she was no longer at the centre of attention and people had other things to think about, and she could again withdraw to the comfort of her own invisibility.

~✥~

The one eating listlessly was Cecilia, who was wondering why she was still thinking about the doctor's beard and hands, while the conversation flowed around her without, for once, tripping over her interpolated comments.

~✥~

The one eating with great pleasure was Ispettore Artistico, because he was proud of how his work was coming along and equally proud, unlike Signorina Barbarici, of being the centre of attention, even though he was not terribly impressed by the food. That might have been explained by the fact that for every dish emerging from Parisina's kitchen, it was noted which was the inspector's plate and an extra handful of salt was added.

~✥~

The one whom it was quite a surprise to see eating was Baronessa Speranza, who looked about her as she ate, aware of the fact that once again the house had resisted the revolutionary assault of the mob.

~✥~

The one eating placidly was Signor Ciceri, who was actually the hero of the moment in a way, a fact which pleased him greatly.

~✥~

The one eating with little birdlike bites was Signorina Cosima Bonaiuti Ferro, who was wondering if it might be better to take her supposed suitor for a walk in the woods tomorrow or to keep the pond with the Japanese carp as a destination, and look how heartily he eats and how manly he is, or should she suggest they take a tour of the estate in the trap, of course the road will be quite muddy but perhaps it's better that way because if the trap stops where I tell the coachman to stop then ha ha hah that would be a laugh, etc., etc., sorry if we cut her off here but following Signorina Cosimo's stream of consciousness might give us a headache.

※

The one eating slowly was Signor Pellegrino, because a question was buzzing around in his head and when that happened he found it hard to eat, and he was trying to summon up the courage to ask a question of the inspector but still couldn't, and just when he had decided not to ask it he heard his own voice say to the inspector, "So what will happen now, Ispettore?"

"What do you mean, Signor Artusi?"

"Well, you know, about the girl . . . I mean, what will happen to her?"

Lapo laughed. "Why, do you sell rope as well as silk?"

"I don't follow you, Signorino Lapo."

"Well, I assume she'll be hanged, as befits a murderess. We're in Italy now, and if there's at least one thing we can thank that unification nonsense for, it's the fact that we're able to hang murderers again. Isn't that so, Ispettore?"

"No, it isn't, Signorino Lapo." The inspector wiped his chin (it isn't right to speak about certain subjects with your chin greasy with sauce) and explained: "The new Zanardelli penal code does not prescribe the death penalty for any kind of offence, thus falling in line with the Grand Duchy of Tuscany, the only region of Italy as you rightly observe where such a penalty was long ago abolished."

"So we don't have the right to hang murderers?"

"I'm sorry, Signorino Lapo, but I fear not. If you really haven't had enough of corpses and want to see someone give up the ghost to Our Lord according to the law, you will have to wait for the next war."

"But that's absurd. So now if someone kills someone else, not only can he not be executed, we also have to take care of him. And you call that progress?"

"No, Signorino Lapo. I call it the law. As to whether or not it is progress, that is not for me to say."

"In any case," said the dowager baroness, making the only gesture that was still allowed her, in other words, opening her mouth, "it is unlikely that the situation will improve now that the government is again in the hands of Signor Crispi."

"I gather, Baronessa," said the inspector, "that Signor Crispi does not inspire confidence in you."

"I don't see how he could. He's a socialist, born in Sicily to parents who, or so I've been told, were not even Sicilians, but Albanians. A person of loose morals, who maintains three families at the same time, and when he's not busy with affairs of state spends his time making children."

"That's his private life though," said the doctor. "In affairs of government, he seems to be tireless and unequalled. In his first term, he passed more laws in six months than Depretis did in all his terms. He speaks constantly in Parliament, and spurs his party to work for unity."

The dinner guests looked at one another for a moment with a touch of dismay in their eyes.

It was well known that when the doctor, already quite prolix by nature, started talking about socialism and government you couldn't shut him up. In fact the only way to reduce him to silence would have been to throw him out of the house. But that seemed less feasible now, after he had treated the baron, which was why most of those at the table (who, by the way, did not care a fig about politics) were overcome with anxiety.

"Just now, you were talking about the penal code: May I remind you that the Zanardelli code that people are talking about was actually passed in the early months of the Crispi government? And it was at last a code based on humanitarian principles, which mentions the divisibility of punishment, not a collection of laws drawn up specially to execute whoever commits an offence, and is equally applicable to all the regions of the kingdom. It is thanks to this that we can at last call ourselves a truly united country, by God. But you know . . ."

From the end of the table came a sudden snort, a kind of strangled laugh, as if it had remained entangled in the imposing whiskers belonging to the man responsible.

"Are you alright, Signor Artusi?"

Artusi made an affirmative sign with his hand, then turned red in the face and began to move his head up and down like a big turkey.

"Oh, my God, did a bone stick in your throat?" said Signorina Cosima anxiously, rising from her chair.

Artusi nodded.

"Wait, here I am . . . Please remain calm and don't move a muscle. The best thing to do in this case . . . If you'll allow me to give you a few pats on the back . . ."

At the idea, perhaps, of being touched by Signorina Cosima, Artusi had such a violent hiccup that the trapped morsel broke free of his illustrious gullet and went down the right way, thus sparing the dinner guests the inconvenience of two deaths in the same weekend. Then he knocked back a large glass of water with great pleasure while the gathering, heartened by this diversion which had strangled the doctor's speech at birth, clustered around him, full of concern.

"Did you get it out?"

"Oh, my poor dear."

"Are you feeling better now?"

"Can you breathe freely?"

"Here, have some more water. Little sips, please."

Artusi obeyed, while Signorina Cosima looked at him with amorous anxiety.

"Please forgive me, I'm mortified. I became distracted because I was so absorbed and interested in our doctor's speech that . . ."

Oh, no, please don't say that. You managed to silence him, and now you're giving him the chance to start all over again.

"I thought you were overcome with a fit of laughter," said Lapo wickedly.

"I had the same impression," concurred Gaddo.

That'll teach you to mind your own business, and next time you can choke in peace.

Artusi mumbled for a moment, then resumed, "Well, the thing is, the doctor was saying that, with the enactment of the new penal code, thanks to the work of Crispi and Zanardelli, ours would finally be a united country."

"I gather you do not agree."

"Trees don't grow from the top down, Dottore Bertini."

"I beg your pardon?"

Watch out, Pellegrino.

Artusi was a shy person, that much was true, but especially when he was young, there had been two specific kinds of situation in which he lost all restraint and became inflamed with passion to such a point that it was difficult to hold him back. The second situation in which this loss of self-control occurred was in political discussions.

As a member of Giovine Italia and a fervent Mazzinian, our bewhiskered friend from Romagna had held the same principles that animated the doctor. But now, having lived long and seen much, he knew that the ideals of which people speak are so elevated that the man who follows them, because of always looking upwards, often does not see where he is putting his feet.

And when he talked to young idealists, Artusi often lost his temper.

This time, being at a nobleman's table, he immediately calmed down.

"I do not dispute that to be united a country must have laws in common, and that is a great goal to aim for. I merely observe that trees don't grow from the top down. It takes time, fertiliser, a yardstick. This country has consisted since time immemorial of two large, unrelated sections, and to claim that they can become a single country with a snap of the fingers, just by passing laws, strikes me, frankly, as too much to hope."

"Signor Artusi is right," Lapo cut in. "We are one country, the South is another. There was no need to burden us with such backward provinces. People who organise subversive movements, like those Fasci who want a socialist revolution and have put the country to fire and sword."

"Forgive me, Signorino Lapo, but that's not what I meant at all. I hope our country will become one, I truly do. What I'm trying to say is that using the force of the law to unite two such different regions isn't the right way."

"Well, as far as I'm concerned, I really don't see the need," said Lapo. "We're as different as oil and water. We couldn't mix even if we wanted to."

In the silence that followed, while Ispettore Artistico tried to establish the right attitude to adopt towards the young fool – indifference, a show of authority, hitting him in the mouth with a tray – Artusi laughed and wiped his moustaches with a professorial air.

"What are you eating, Signorino Lapo? I mean, with what is your fish dressed?"

"With mayonnaise. Would you like to taste it?"

"No, thank you. Do you know what mayonnaise is composed of?"

"I have no idea. I'm sure there's egg. And lemon, I think."

"Exactly right. Now, tell me, do you know how it's made?"

Silence. Cooking is woman's work, said Lapo's eyes. The only thing a real man does in the kitchen is to creep up behind the cook and . . . well, no need to continue.

"Then please allow me a brief culinary digression. Mayonnaise is a stable emulsion of oil in a watery base, constituted by lemon juice and vinegar. In practice, it's like a whole lot of tiny drops of oil spread through a watery base. The stability of such drops is given by a component of egg yolk known as lecithin."

Artusi drew two or three drops in the air.

"Lecithin is a molecule which is believed to be shaped like a kind of tadpole – forgive the crudeness of this explanation – which has a hydrophilic head, that is, a head which melts in water, and a lipophilic tail, that is, a tail which melts in oils and fats. When we beat water and oil together, the drops which form are stabilised by the presence of these small tadpoles, which arrange themselves with their tails inside the drop and with their heads in the water, thus anchoring the surface of the drop in its own watery environment and avoiding the emulsion breaking up and the whole thing turning back to oil floating in water."

"Well explained," said the doctor.

"Indeed," said Gaddo. "But what of it?"

"What of it? Simply that to make mayonnaise we need to proceed calmly and methodically. If we put everything together

125

and then beat it, nasty lumps form. In the trade, it is said to have curdled. We have to put the egg yolks in a bowl, beat them a little, and then slowly add a trickle of oil and stir with a spoon until everything is well mixed. Very slowly at first, almost drop by drop, and then towards the end we can increase the speed with which we add the oil, but not too much. Then, at the end, we add lemon juice or vinegar or even, as the French do, mustard."

"And what are you trying to get at with this explanation?"

"What I'm trying to get at is mayonnaise. Something that isn't water and isn't oil, and yet is even more precious than the components with which we start, with a thick, creamy texture all of its own, even though it is obtained by mixing liquids. Partly for that reason, and partly because of its versatility, which allows us to flavour it as we please, it is rightly considered the queen of sauces. But it takes patience and method to obtain it, we have to go carefully and slowly. It can't be done with brute force. And we need something that persuades water and oil to stay together, that works on both in the same way, especially as, if the mayonnaise curdles, the only way to save it is to add another egg yolk, preferably hard-boiled. There is no point adding lots of salt, or adding more water, or more oil. That won't get us any-where."

Dinner was over, and the gathering had divided first by gender (men to the billiard room, women to the sitting room) and then by birth: Lapo and Gaddo had decided to abandon the castle, to take the trap and go to Bolgheri to cheer themselves up a little after the terrible weekend, and then return nicely rested to their usual activities – that is, although with differing talents and attitudes, to not doing a damned thing from morning to evening.

The non-nobles, apart from the doctor, who had gone to see how the baron was, had remained in the billiard room, not so much because they especially liked each other and wanted to be together as because Ispettore Artistico had expressly asked both of them if he could have a quick word with them.

Alone now, as Ciceri idly sent balls bouncing across the green table, the inspector said, "I'm going to need some explanations from you, if you don't mind."

"At your disposal, Ispettore," said Signor Ciceri.

"Would you both be so kind as to tell me the exact purpose of your visit here. In the most detailed and exhaustive way possible. Will you begin, Signor Artusi?"

"As you wish, Ispettore. You may know that I enjoy a certain fame as a gourmet, having some time ago published a small book of recipes. Well, this spring I went to Montecatini to take the waters, as I do every year, and I lodged at the Locanda Maggiore, as did our host, the baron. On that occasion we started reminiscing about how different the spa had been when both of us had started going there, since the baron, too, was an enthusiastic visitor to the place. I should explain, Ispettore, that when I went to Montecatini for the first time there was no other accommodation but the Locanda dei Frati, apart from a woman named Carmela Calugi who rented out rooms. The water was free, and the village peaceful: not like now, when there are taverns, hotels, theatres, and every kind of entertainment. Mind you, I'm not saying that's a bad thing. When—"

The inspector raised his hand to interrupt Artusi.

Although having neither the moustache nor the glittering eye nor the bony hand of Coleridge's Ancient Mariner, the inspector was able to recognise the birth pangs of a never-ending story, and did not want to spend half the evening listening to the story of Artusi's youth.

"Forgive me, Signor Artusi, but would you mind getting to the point?"

"I'm sorry, Ispettore, but this is the point. The baron talked to me about how the hotel situation had changed over the years, and I could only concur. To cut a long story short, he told me of a plan of his – in brief, to use part of his castle as a hotel for visitors and tourists of a certain lineage – and he asked me for my opinion. Somewhat impudently perhaps, I told him that, having never lodged with him, I did not know what to say."

Artusi picked up a ball and threw it towards one of the cushions, sending it unwittingly into the hole.

"In truth, the idea struck me as a little odd. I mean, Ispettore, would you expect tourists to come to the moors of the Maremma, filled as they are with marshes and mosquitoes? By way of reply, he told me I was right and invited me to spend some time here. As a lover of good living, he said. You'll try my food, my rooms, my stables . . ."

The inspector shuddered at the thought of the poor horse.

". . . and then you'll tell me what you think. What was I to do,

Ispettore? So here I am. To be cynical, I have to admit that so far I certainly haven't been bored."

"Thank you. And what about you, Signor Ciceri?"

"Well, Ispettore, there isn't much to say. The baron made my acquaintance in Florence, where he visited my photographic studio and asked me if it was possible to photograph his castle and take a few pictures of the hunt and the life of the place. The offer was an attractive one, and the price favourable. And here I am."

"I understand. Well, gentlemen, there is nothing else to say. It has been a long day, and we all deserve a little amusement."

Smiling, the inspector went and took a cue from the rack. Simultaneously Artusi rose from his chair, also smiling.

"You will excuse me, Ispettore, but these games do nothing for me. When I'm at a table I prefer to be sitting rather than bending."

With that paunch of yours, you'd need a cue that was three metres long even to reach the table.

"Apart from anything else," concluded Artusi, smoothing his unkempt whiskers, "I must call on the cook."

"Is there a little hanky-panky going on?" asked Signor Ciceri mischievously as he took a cue for himself.

"Oh, no, come on. The cook must be sixty if she's a day."

And what about you? said Ciceri's eyebrows.

"I mentioned to the baronessa that I know the recipe for a special soup for the sick, substantial and nutritious but not heavy on the stomach, and she asked me to teach it to the cook so that she could make it for her son."

"Oh, these Italian mothers," replied Ciceri distractedly. "They're

129

all the same, baronessas or not. Their first concern is that their son eats enough for three people. Everything else is of lesser importance."

"How right you are. Well, goodnight, gentlemen."

"Goodnight to you."

"We need a way to mark the score," said the inspector after Artusi had left the room, applying chalk to the tip of his cue.

"Isn't there a movable scoreboard?"

"I don't see any. Never mind, we'll use a sheet of paper. There are some over there, behind you."

Turning, Ciceri took a sheet from a writing desk of rare ugliness and divided it into two columns with a stroke of the pen. On the right he wrote *Ispettore* and on the left *Ciceri*.

"Perfect," said the inspector. "Shall we begin?"

❦

Halfway through the game, by which time various numbers had already been written in the columns on both sides of the sheet, the inspector took off his jacket (it isn't easy to play billiards with your jacket on) and as he did so he uncovered a sheet of paper sticking out from his inside pocket. Noticing it, he took it out with an innocent air.

"Ah, I almost forgot. Do you know anything about this letter, Signor Ciceri?"

The sheet of paper glided from the inspector's hand onto the billiard table.

Signor Ciceri picked it up. And turned pale.

"Signor Ciceri?"

Silence.

"I have the feeling you recognise it. In fact, I'd even hazard a guess that you wrote it. You see, the figures on the date are written in a very particular way. They look rather like the ones you've put down on the score sheet."

Putting the paper down, Ciceri looked at the inspector. "Alright. What can I say? Yes, I know this letter. In fact, I wrote it myself."

"I see. Given that you are being so reasonable, perhaps you could tell me the whole story."

With regained calm, Signor Ciceri put down his cue and began. "It's quite simple. One day this fellow comes into my studio and tells me he's the Barone di Roccapendente and that he got my address from his dear friend Barone Caradonna. He tells me that he needs money for some urgent business of his and that he doesn't have a large enough sum at his disposal. I reassure him that I may be able to lend him, out of friendship obviously, the sum he's looking for, and I ask him to come back the following morning."

"Of course. You needed to find out something about him. Guarantees. Isn't that so?"

Signor Ciceri smiled, with a smile that the inspector knew well: that of the bastard who is telling you you have understood perfectly well but can't prove a damn thing.

"The following day I get him the money, and he swears to me that within a month he'll be back in Florence to honour his commitment. That happened on the tenth of April, in other words, about two and a half months ago. Obviously, friendship is all very well, but ten thousand lire isn't chicken feed."

"Obviously. So how much is your friendship worth, fifteen per cent?"

"Come on, Ispettore, do I strike you as someone who'd squeeze his customers?"

Bold as brass, this Ciceri. And they talk about Southerners! This fellow could give points to the worst *camorristi* I've ever met.

"In any case, the baron was as good as his word. Yesterday, when we got to the village, we made a little detour to the office of Signor Corradini, the gentleman who keeps the betting book at the local racecourse. The baron withdrew his winnings and was finally able to unburden his conscience of this debt of his."

"A genuine act of charity on your part. And what about the whole photography story?"

"Come on, Ispettore, you wouldn't expect me to present myself at my friend's house and ask for money? That wouldn't be delicate. It can be difficult, though, to get an invitation. You know, some of these noblemen who are down on their luck have families, and often these families don't look kindly on the invitation of a nobody without even a quarter noble blood. But if the guest in question is an artist, things change, don't you think?"

"And don't you think the baron will have no difficulty in telling me that you came here to demand money from him?"

"Why should he do that? He's already had a lot of unpleasant things happen to him this weekend. Are you so sure he'd tell you something like that, now or later?"

No, you bastard. You're right. The baron won't say a word, like all those who end up dealing with usurers. For now I can't do anything to you, but I'm damned if I'm going to forget your name and where you live.

From the diary of Pellegrino Artusi

Sunday, 18 June, 1895

So many unexpected things have befallen me today that I would find it hard to write them all down. I find myself the guest in a manor house where the butlers are murdered, which does not usually happen to me. This morning the master of the house was shot, and that was followed by a tremendous hubbub; this afternoon the culprit was apprehended, and turned out to be none other than the young Juno from whom I received confidences.

If it is true that diversion comes from divertire, *to change direction, to do or experience things to which we are not accustomed, I must admit that this weekend has been genuinely diverting.*

This evening, after dinner, I went to find the cook in her realm, to show her how to make soup for convalescents; I found her in a state of great agitation. Immediately she assailed me with a stream of the most indecent abuse, which offended me more than a little. But then, listening more carefully, I realised that the stranger on whom she wished various intestinal pathologies was not myself, but Ispettore Artistico. Brandishing a ladle like a weapon, she asked me if I too happened to be one of those who were saying that Agatina was a murderess and should be hanged; to which I replied that I did not think that at all.

This appeased her somewhat: I told her why I was there, and after five minutes we were chatting away like two old friends, so much so that I took the liberty of asking her a favour. If I prepare the soup, I said, and you prepare your gypsy pie (such is the name of the tuna-based delicacy I could not get out of my mind), each of us, by observing, will learn from the other what to do, and in the meantime you can tell me about Agatina – since I had understood that this was her prime concern.

So we got to work; she began by peeling a yellow pepper over the fire, and then went and put in a pan some celery cut into large pieces, to which she added the pepper in little strips and olives without the stones. In the meantime, she brought about two deci-litres of milk to the boil and soaked some slices of stale bread in it.

After putting some tuna in oil into the pan, crumbling it with her hands, she mixed it until the concoction had absorbed all the fat. Then she added the soaked bread and two eggs, mixed every-thing together and put it in the oven.

While she was doing this, she told me how this dish had been taught to her by actual gypsies, years earlier, when her father was a horse trader who had dealings with these nomads. Such dealings were intense, and often, being a matter of business and moreover with people of a fiery nature, the negotiations led to quarrels, which died down as easily as they had flared up, and it was then necessary to make peace: and ever since the world began peace has been made at the table.

Seeing that stew of so many different things, I found it hard to believe that the delicate and yet flavoursome dish I had been served two days earlier could emerge from such a hotchpotch; but I was prepared to wait and see. While we waited, I learned many things about Agatina and Teodoro. I learned that the two of them had been due to marry, and as a matter of some urgency, indeed, given that they had found themselves in that situation that often occurs when one is young and impatient.

All these things the cook told me in that sad tone the common people often use to talk about matters of life, almost as if telling them in a heart-breaking manner ennobles them in some way; she told me, for example, that on the day of his passing Teodoro had been going around beating his chest with his hand and telling everyone that he had over his heart something that would change his life. When the poor fellow was found dead, over his heart he had a worn wallet, in which the only thing found was a portrait of Agatina.

Now that I am writing, I realise that Agatina's guilt, even though proved, torments me; almost as if, having seen that young beauty and having received her smiles and her confidences, I had become convinced that I had to be her protector in some way, unable as I was to be anything else for reasons of age. I suppose it is true that the older we get the more foolish we become and yet, without these instincts, it is likely that the human race would not have lasted as long as it has. The instinct for nutrition and the sexual instinct are necessary to us, since without them we wouldn't last long: and yet they are thought of as vile subjects, and when we talk about them in drawing rooms there is the risk we will be considered depraved.

Anyway, the time passed and the dish emerged: which, in spite of the ingredients that had seemed to me an unlikely patchwork, was just as I remembered it, and perhaps even better. I served myself just enough of it not to have stomach problems in the course of the night, and I wrapped a little of it to give to my furry friends, who are appreciating it greatly as I write.

Well, tomorrow at last we will return to Florence, our good friend and sweet companion, and will leave this unfortunate affair behind us, these corpses and these rampant old maids; and I hope to read about murders only in books, and nothing more.

Sunday night

The rhythm of his steps on the pavement left no room for doubt.

Gaddo was beside himself.

Usually, Gaddo walked with slow, irregular steps, stopping often to think, to listen, to fantasise. Now, instead, he was almost marching, at a regular, quite rapid pace, with his feet sinking into the ground and making the paving stones grate beneath his soles.

And to think that the evening had started well. The servant girl who had tried to kill his father had been arrested, partly due to his own intervention, or at least so he thought. And he had found the inspiration for a new poem as he lay between the ears of corn, trying to catch his breath, having frittered away his whole capital of oxygen in the thirty-six metres he had run after Agatina.

Just as he was trying to regain his breath, Gaddo had found himself looking up at the sky.

A clear, cloudless sky.

A very high sky, without points of reference.

A measureless sky, and yet so real.

My God, what an idea.

~~❧~~

He and his brother had decided to give themselves a free evening in Bolgheri, and while Lapo went to his usual tavern, Gaddo had begun wandering the back alleys of the village, thinking about his new poem.

A measureless sky. A sky so real. What else rhymes with real?

Steel, of course. But the sky isn't like steel. Never mind. *Where the sky seems so real, and turquoise turns to steel* . . . Not bad, eh? Yes, but it isn't true. The higher you look in the sky, the clearer the sky is. What a bore, when poetry has to take reality into account. It would be so good otherwise.

And, lost in his verses, he had continued to walk. Until, at a certain point, his heart (already sensitive on its own account and now overexcited by the new poem) had begun beating even louder. Because a few metres away, at the end of the alley, a majestic figure had appeared. A leonine head, a thick beard, a heavy, alert gait that everyone in these parts knew well.

Giosue Carducci.

Gaddo had almost frozen as the poet advanced slowly and majestically along the narrow alley, calmly looking about him. Furtively, Gaddo had let the imposing figure go by, wondering if he should greet him or not, if he should show him that he had recognised him or not, if it might not be best to come right out with it and say good evening, Senator, forgive my boldness but . . .

But . . .

What is he doing?

While Gaddo stood there motionless, watching, the poet had stopped outside a door and studied it sternly for a few seconds. Then, having found it well suited, he had unbuttoned his trousers with some difficulty and begun calmly to empty his bladder, with his head up in the indifferent manner that characterises those accustomed to peeing in the open air.

Gaddo had remained transfixed.

After some ten seconds, the noble scion had approached the urinating poet and looked at him in astonishment.

Carducci did not react in any way.

At this point, Gaddo had exploded. "What on earth are you doing?" he had said, his voice trembling with anger and surprise.

Completely undisturbed, the poet had uttered the following lines:

> *My friend, can you not see what is before*
> *Your eyes? Why, I am peeing on a door.*
> *I pee where'er I wish and when it suits,*
> *I pee on flowerbeds and on the rocks.*
> *I pee on moneybags and on fresh shoots,*
> *I pee in Vatican realms whome'er it shocks;*
> *And if you linger there to brown me off*
> *I'll pee right on your face as soon as cough.*

And, having finished this verse pronouncement, he had buttoned himself up and turned imperturbably on his heels, leaving poor Gaddo motionless and stunned.

~❧~

And so, when he had recovered, Gaddo had set off for home.

Four kilometres on foot, but then anger is a fuel not to be underestimated. Anger at having made a complete fool of himself in front of his own idol. Anger at realising that, of the two, he was certainly not the one who had behaved badly, but rather that disgusting old man who had started peeing in a doorway without batting an eyelid, and yet he himself, the guiltless young man, was the one who had felt embarrassed.

Anger, above all, at having discovered that his idol was, at bottom, a man like any other. And this anger, as happens with feelings to which we cannot give vent, had accumulated as he approached home, rising and swelling in expectation of a target on which to take it out.

As we are in a novel, it would seem strange at this point if the poor disillusioned nobleman did not find an innocent element on which to pour out the above-mentioned anger. It will therefore come as no surprise to learn that, as soon as he got home, the first thing Gaddo did was to trip over the dog Briciola.

❧

"What's going on?"

"How should I know?"

Sounds of running footsteps, canine growls, heavy breathing.

"Who's there?"

"Oh my God, it isn't thieves, is it?"

Sudden silence, the sound of a plate breaking, a dog barking, a man's voice saying something like "bloody animal".

"Cecilia, what's going on?"

"I don't know, Nonna. It's quite dark. Oh, I'm so sorry."

"It's alright, Signorina. We need a candle."

No sooner said than done. From the room at the end of the corridor emerged a figure in a white nightshirt and a cotton cap with a pompom, holding a candlestick with a lighted candle, kept cautiously at a distance from his bushy beard.

In the flickering light it was now possible to make out:

a) Cecilia in a cotton nightdress and a dressing gown, barefoot and sleepy-eyed.

b) Cosima Bonaiuti Ferro in what looked like a coat of chain mail, weighing about fifteen kilos, with matching cotton socks, clearly bought from the spring–summer catalogue of the well-bred old maid.

c) Signorina Barbarici dressed God knows how, because from the door of her room only her head and haggard neck were visible, like a postmodern tortoise.

d) Pellegrino Artusi in a silk dressing gown and leather slippers in the Moorish style.

While the doctor approached the rest of the company, the two adversaries, in other words, Gaddo and the dog Briciola, had come up the stairs. The dog, highly menacing in demeanour however small in bulk, was barking and growling and backing away from Gaddo, who bounced back a few centimetres with every bark because of the displacement of air.

A candelabra in hand, shoeless, sweaty, hair dishevelled, and as angry as a pig in January, Gaddo was advancing inexorably towards the animal.

"Oh, Gadduccio, what are you doing?"

Surprised by the light and the number of people present, Gaddo looked at his aunt for a moment as if weighing up whether to change target, then threw the candelabra furiously on the floor.

"What am I doing? I'm coming back to my own home, God Almighty, and the first thing I do is trip over this cur of yours, this poor excuse for a dog! No sooner have I got back on my feet when this beast bites my ankle!"

"But you frightened the poor thing. He was asleep, and you stepped on him. Poor Briciola, what are these bad people doing to you? Bad, yes, Gaddo was really bad, come, Briciola, come . . ."

And Signorina Cosima walked lovingly towards her pet, which was continuing to show its teeth and gums to Gaddo.

Unfortunately, on coming out, Artusi had left open the door of his room, inside which were not just one but two cats, which, woken by all that commotion, had reacted in different ways. Timorous by nature, Sibillone had taken shelter under the bed, while Bianchino, being more enterprising, had come out into the corridor and had immediately identified the enemy.

As the signorina approached, the cat swelled like a ball and started to puff, then, estimating that the enemy weighed less than it did and did not have sharp claws, launched its attack.

The moments that followed were convulsive.

In the middle of the corridor, the two animals formed a growling and miaowing ball of fur, while the onlookers watched powerless.

As Artusi tried to call his own animal to order in Romagnol dialect, Signorina Bonaiuti Ferro went straight to the furry spheroid and tried to resolve the situation by kicking the cat, which was on top of the dog and brutalising it. But, as the signorina aimed the kick, the two animals reversed their positions, so that

Signorina Cosima's foot impacted with vigour against her own pet, bending it like a horseshoe and projecting it against the wall, which it hit with a yelp.

Gaddo had stood there transfixed during this scene, but now he let out a strangled snort and began to laugh.

After a moment, they all laughed.

All of them, including Signorina Barbarici with her tortoise-like neck, Artusi with his military whiskers and the doctor with his solemn beard.

All of them, except Signorina Cosima, who had turned, red in the face, to look at Artusi.

"You . . . You . . ."

"Forgive me, Signorina Cosima, but—"

Signorina Cosima pointed at the cat, which was running back into his room. "You and your animals! It's all your fault! And here was I, imagining that . . ."

"Signorina, I'm speechless," said Artusi laughing, "but you see—"

"Don't you dare come near me! And don't you ever say another word to me, you savage, you disgusting fat man! I never want to see you or speak to you again, do you understand? Never! Briciola, come here, my darling . . ."

Monday morning

I have to find the right way to say it. And that isn't at all easy.

As he walked up and down the lawn, trying to prepare a speech that might seem both authoritative and courteous, Ispettore Artistico cursed the doctor.

Everything had been going well up until a few hours earlier. He had the guilty party, he had the motive, he had an almost perfect theoretical reconstruction of the crime. He was ready to go back home, have that good long sleep he had been dreaming about for two days, and go to the Commissioner the following morning with all the paperwork in his hand. Crime, investigation, solution, arrest. He was not too worried about proof: the photograph showing Agatina as she aimed at the baron's august back was more than enough.

But unfortunately Ispettore Artistico had discovered for himself that very night (some years, in other words, before the birth of a child named Karl Popper) that a correctly constructed theory is a theory that can be falsified. It does not matter how many elements there are in its favour: all it takes is a single, simple, really stupid counter-example and the theory falls to pieces.

The inspector was there at the billiard table, feeling quite clever, thinking over all the aspects of the affair as he played. The case had been solved. The baron, that crafty old dog, trifles with the housemaid (who could blame him?) and unwittingly conceives an illegitimate child. The noble gentleman can deny it as much as he wants, but that's the long and the short of it. Having realised the gravity of the situation, the housemaid goes to the baron and asks for money. There is no way: the baron is already being measured by his tailor for new patches to his trousers, he is forced to deny money to his official sons, and now he has to give money to the housemaid? So the housemaid is sent packing – told in fact to go and do to herself what he has previously done to her. Agatina decides to take her revenge and do away with the baron. The first time, thanks to the designated victim's stomachache and Teodoro's greed, she misses her target in the most disastrous way possible. The second time, we all know about. Does that add up? Yes, it seems to me that it does.

As the inspector was making the ivory ball bounce off the cushion, putting it in position for a strike that would send the ball against three cushions one after the other, the doctor had entered the room.

"The baron is much better, it seems to me. His blood pressure had risen for a reason I cannot explain, given that he lost a fair amount of blood, but now everything appears to have gone back to normal."

"Well, I'm pleased. And what about us?"

"I've brought you what you requested. My expert opinion, which is that the liquid in the glass found by the body contained the alkaloid known as atropine."

Couldn't he be a little less pompous? He's clearly the kind of person who's determined to show us how many words he knows.

The inspector smiled like someone who, after poisoning his mother-in-law, receives news that the old lady isn't feeling well.

"In the liquid contained in the bottle, on the other hand, I did not find the slightest trace either of this or any other alkaloid."

The ball hit by the inspector, after missing the yellow ball, described an elegant rhombus and ended in the hole.

"Wait. Stop. In the bottle no, but in the glass yes?"

"Precisely."

"And how can you be so sure?"

"I added bismuth iodide and potassium to the solution after treating it appropriately, even though the wine, being acid by nature, did not require such a procedure. The liquid in the glass showed the formation of an orange-coloured precipitate, while . . ."

Instead of giving scientific explanations, the doctor could have justified his statement by admitting that, once the absence of toxin in the port had been verified, he had also empirically verified the organoleptic properties of the wine by knocking back a couple of glasses with a nice piece of sweet cake, and all things considered was still alive. But Dottore Bertini was one of those who consider that science must be listened to and give credence, full stop, even when a perfectly vulgar example would not come amiss.

"Spare me the scientific masturbation. Where did you get the idea for the iodide?"

"But my dear Ispettore, it's the procedure prescribed by

Dragendorff in his treatise on forensic chemistry, *Die gerichtlich-chemische Ermittelung von Giften*".

Ispettore Artistico was ready to question anything that was said by the doctor, but being very sensitive to the principle of authority and profoundly Italian in spirit, he did not feel that he was in a position to challenge the dictates of a book written by a luminary with such a sonorous name, and in German to boot.

"I understand."

And, unfortunately, it was true.

~☙~

Once the family had all gathered for breakfast (apart from the baron, who was still only so-so, the dowager baroness, who always had breakfast in bed, and Signorina Barbarici, who, since the baroness was still in bed, had gone to ground in the cellar with her beloved bottle of absinthe, given that benzodiazepines had not yet been invented), the inspector asked for permission to make a brief speech.

"Ladies and gentlemen, I'm truly sorry to have to inform you that you will have to bear my presence here for a little while longer."

What?

"New details have emerged which make further investigation necessary."

"Ispettore, is this a joke?"

"I never joke in the exercise of my duty, Signorino Lapo. I must therefore ask you and your guests to be available for—"

"But this is outrageous! I shan't allow you to keep these people hostage! You have done your work, you have browned all of us off, and now you want to continue? What is it, are you intending to work on the cook?"

While Lapo was speaking, Gaddo kept his gaze fixed on his plate.

"Signorino Lapo, I have asked you in the most civil manner possible to detain your guests. I could have done so with the full weight of my authority."

"Lapo, I think the inspector is right. Our duty—"

"Shut up!"

And Lapo accompanied this command, as he often did, with an open-handed slap on the back of his brother's neck. This was where he made a mistake.

"Ispettore!" he said, rising to his feet. "Following a criminal incident, we consented to accommodate you."

He made a mistake because sometimes even the weak and the cowardly, when they are humiliated in public and in front of people they respect, find the strength to react.

"Following the precepts imposed on us by our rank, we have listened to you and have allowed you to carry out your investigation among our family and servants. Now will you do us the pleasure—"

What pleasure Lapo hoped to obtain from the inspector was not to become clear, however, because while the arrogant young fellow was making his triumphant speech, Gaddo had picked up a plate of the finest Wedgwood, and now, after weighing it carefully and appreciating its manufacture, ground it into his brother's gums with a graceful but resolute gesture.

There was silence for a moment.

As Gaddo again brought his gaze to rest on his own plate, Lapo lifted his right hand to his mouth and took out a bloodstained fistful of fragments of porcelain and assorted front teeth.

A fight ensued.

~~~

"I asked to see you, Ispettore, to apologise for the shameful behaviour of my grandsons, and to ask you to draw over the pitiful scene you witnessed an equally pitiful veil."

Standing in the bedroom of the dowager baroness, who seemed the only person to have remain impassive and impervious to all the terrible things that had happened, the inspector listened in silence.

"I realise that you are only doing your duty, and I ask you to take into account the effort that we, too, are making, some more than others, to assist you. We are not accustomed to this kind of thing."

"Nobody is accustomed to having crimes committed in their houses, Baronessa."

"That is not what I am referring to, Ispettore. We are not accustomed to having to account to anyone for our conduct. We are barons, and we do not normally defer to anyone below the rank of count."

Ispettore Artistico forced himself not to smile.

"When he was small and had got up to some mischief or other, my son was in the habit of hiding in the most inaccessible places. He would disappear, and could not be found for days.

Then, one day, the estate manager discovered where he was hiding, and told my husband, the late baron. My son was punished: he had done something stupid, after all, and was sent to bed without dinner. The following morning, while the estate manager was saddling his horse for him, my son looked at him and said, 'In a few years, Amidei, I'll be Barone. Bear that in mind from now on.'"

The inspector said nothing.

"Do you understand?" the baroness went on after a few moments. "We have been raised in a state of impunity, in our own world of which we were either masters or would become masters. This certainty has always cradled us. We have never made an effort to see what was beyond the cradle, or even thought to wonder if there was anything. And my son is no exception."

A few more seconds passed. The baroness sighed, while the inspector remained silent.

"Well, Ispettore, we have detained you far too long. I think it is time for you to get back to your work."

"I am most grateful to you. My respects, Baronessa."

❧

"Are you going out, Signor Artusi?

"Oh, Ispettore. Yes, in fact I was about to go for a stroll in the woods."

"Not to escape our surveillance, I hope."

"What do you mean? Oh, no, Ispettore, not at all. The fact is, it has rained quite a lot lately, and we are near a chestnut wood. So I thought of looking for mushrooms and making them into an omelette when I return home."

As well as getting out of this madhouse, said Artusi's eyes to the inspector, who understood.

"Well, I can't see any harm in that. In fact, if you don't mind, I'll keep you company."

"I'd be delighted. Will you take a basket?"

⚜

"So, the mushrooms are good in June, are they?"

"Excellent, Ispettore. The weather is dry, and the mushroom contains less water. Its nitrogenous properties and its essential oils are more concentrated and have a more intense flavour."

Their eyes on the ground in search of mushrooms, the two men talked of this and that, avoiding as far as possible the subject of what was happening in the castle. But sooner or later . . .

"Ispettore . . ."

"Go on."

"I should like to know, Ispettore, when I will be allowed to go back to Florence. You see, mushrooms should be eaten fresh, and I'd like to . . ."

Continuing to search in the undergrowth with sticks – the inspector had grown up in a place full of snakes – Artistico replied, "If it were up to me, Signor Artusi, I would let you go immediately, since you are no longer on the list of suspects. But in order not to wrong anyone I prefer all the guests to remain here for as long as possible."

"I see. And why, pray, do you not consider me a suspect?"

The inspector looked at Artusi.

You have to trust someone.

"Last night, Dottore Bertini informed me that the poison was only present in the glass, not in the bottle. Now, I had already previously established with absolute certainty that the glasses like the one used by the baron are kept in a dresser in the same room where the drinks are served. During the period of time that concerns us, the housemaid never entered that room. And the idea that she could have poisoned the glass previously to that must be ruled out. The extract of belladonna would have stained it. Whoever poured the poison into the wine was present in the room at the time of the toast. And that, apart from removing the house-maid as a possible poisoner, *ipso facto* also rules you out."

"I am pleased to hear it, Ispettore."

"I am not quite so pleased. It means I now have to arrest two people, not one. I feel like that mythological character who was forced to roll a stone up a hill, and once he got to the top the stone would plummet back down and he would have to start again from scratch."

"Sisyphus."

"Precisely. And now I don't know what to do."

"Eliminate the impossible. Whatever remains, however improbable, must be the truth."

What on earth is he talking about?

"That's what the main character in the book I'm reading says," explained Artusi by way of justification.

"Ah, I see. A bit general, though, don't you think?"

Artusi said nothing.

153

"To be honest, though, I have already heeded the first part of that advice. It can't have been Agatina. Or you."

Still Artusi said nothing.

"Well, Signor Artusi, don't you feel reassured?"

"I am grateful to you, Ispettore, but I was already well aware that I had not murdered anyone. The few times I have taken the life of a living creature, I have usually cooked it in a sauce soon afterwards, and I do not possess casserole dishes large enough to get humans into them."

The inspector laughed, and even Artusi allowed himself a bewhiskered smile.

"Among other things, there is no evidence that you had any misunderstanding with the baron."

"Indeed not. The most regrettable misunderstanding I have had, I fear, was with Signorina Cosima."

Remembering how he, too, had suffered in the course of his interview with the old maid, the inspector shook his head in sympathy. "Do such misadventures often befall you?" he asked.

"My dear Ispettore, what can I say? My magnetic personality will have to be put under lock and key."

Silence.

"You know, in my youth I certainly did nothing to avoid amorous adventures. There are stories I could tell you! But marriage . . . My poor mother, seeing how inclined I was to court the fair sex, almost begged me to take a wife. For my part, I have always thought that marriage vows are mediaeval dogmas, unnatural obligations that no longer have any *raison d'être* in a rational, progressive environment. In fact, I'd go further: it would be a good idea, in my opinion, for a law to be passed allowing divorce, as has been the case for some time now in the most civilised nations of the world."

Silence.

"What do you think, Ispettore? Will we ever see, in this odd little nation of ours, a law that laughs at dogma and takes account of the man more than the priest?"

Silence.

Pellegrino Artusi turned. The inspector was nowhere to be seen.

⁓❧⁓

Damn. Damn. Damn.

Puffing with annoyance, the inspector was walking towards the castle.

This is the second time that Artusi fellow has shown me the way.

With each step he took, his thoughts became clearer, one piece at a time.

If you eliminate the impossible . . .

If you eliminate the impossible, what remains must be the truth.

If this time everything falls into place, I'll offer you more than lunch, my dear fellow.

Quickly now. As long as my target is in no position to get away.

Monday, don't ask me what time

My God, she's beautiful.

Tousled hair, dark eyes, her expression no longer proud but like that of a wounded beast, which somehow made her all the more beautiful, voluptuous, wild. Pull yourself together, Saverio. You're on duty and she's practically a recent widow. It wouldn't be right.

"How are you feeling, Agatina?"

No reply. Not verbally, at any rate. I'm fine, and I'd be even better if I could get my hands on you. And not the way you hope, you pig.

"Listen to me, Agatina. I have to ask you a few questions. Do you feel up to answering me?"

"No."

It was the first time the inspector had heard Agatina's voice. To describe it as sensual would have been an understatement. Deep and husky, and at the same time feminine, suggestive.

Having said that one word, Agatina lay down on the plank bed in the cell and turned onto her side, away from the inspector, giving him a full, comfortable vision of her posterior.

The inspector could feel his rough regulation trousers clinging to his thighs. He, too, turned away in order to concentrate.

"I think I know why you shot the baron, Agatina."

No reaction.

"And I also think I've understood that, before Saturday morning, you had no reason to wish for the baron's death."

No reaction. Perhaps.

"But between Friday and Saturday something happened. And after it happened, you tried to kill your master. Not before. After. And I wonder why."

Agatina's body had stiffened. This time he was sure.

"But the reason is something I can only imagine. And if you do not confirm it to me and give me some elements of proof, it won't be easy for me to help you."

Agatina relaxed. It won't be easy for *me* to help *you*.

The inspector took a deep breath, sat down and tried to concentrate on the back of the housemaid's neck.

"I'll begin with a very simple question. As far as you know, was Teodoro in the habit of betting on the horses?"

Agatina turned.

I know everything, the inspector's face told her.

Agatina began to weep.

❧

Once he had finished talking to Agatina, Ispettore Artistico quickly summoned Officer Bacci and sent him to Barone Cesaroni with a specific question. To be on the safe side he even wrote it down for him on a sheet of paper, to prevent him from getting hold of the wrong end of his cock (yes, it should be the wrong end of the stick: forgive me for relieving my feelings, this late

157

nineteenth-century language is getting a bit much and after a while you need a change of air). Then he returned to the castle and set off in search of Dottore Bertini.

~~❧~~

Having found the doctor, he asked him a very specific question. To which the doctor replied in his usual exhaustive manner, "Yes, disorders of urination can appear. Generally dependent on all the smooth muscles. And certainly there is a trace of what you say in the urine. The identification of such a drug—"

The doctor had intended to continue, but the inspector cut him short.

"Would you be prepared to repeat in front of witnesses what you have told me?"

"That is a doctor's clear task when summoned to court . . ."

"No, Dottore. I am asking you to confirm what you have just said in the presence of the baron and his family, here, in a short while."

This time it was the doctor's turn to turn red. He swallowed two or three times and looked about him, but he had painted himself into a corner. "Yes, of course," he said in a slightly hoarse voice. "It's my duty."

Then the inspector went to see Amidei. This was the hardest part.

"I don't remember a thing."

"Are you sure, Amidei?"

"I told you. Not a thing."

"Strange. Usually, things that provoke strong emotions are

hard to forget, I think."

"Maybe so."

The inspector sighed. "I understand. You're loyal to your master. Round here you call it honour, don't you? Where I come from, it's called *omertà*."

"I don't know what that means. Never heard the word."

"It means that someone knows perfectly well what he's being asked, but doesn't answer because he's scared."

"I'm not scared of anything."

And that might even be true. Primo Amidei was a man who, if anything, scared other people. Tall and bulky with two shovels instead of hands and a way of looking you straight in the eyes that was a constant threat. The estate manager.

The man who makes sure that everything keeps going.

Today the people we call managers usually do exactly the opposite.

"I'm very pleased for you. So you'll have no objection if I go and ask your mistress directly, will you?"

"I don't know what you're talking about."

There was no way to get another word from him. But for the inspector, who had been born and raised in a place where keeping silent was often the only means of communication, that silence was as good as an answer.

❧

"Baronessa . . ."

"Good day to you, Ispettore. Have you concluded your investigation?"

"Actually I have, Baronessa. I'm waiting for one last reply, and then everything will be done."

"Then we shall never see each other again. I am relieved."

"Careful what you say, Baronessa," said the inspector in an amusingly grumpy manner. "I might still be hidden in that secret hiding place of your son's, the one you told me about this morning."

"You wouldn't enjoy it. And as long as you are on duty, you would not be able to take advantage of it."

"Really? Why?"

"Because that little devil . . ."

The baroness broke off and gave the inspector a look of surprise.

"Because the little devil was in the habit of shutting himself in the cellar, wasn't he?" said the inspector.

Silence is consent.

"And not just that. Correct me if I'm wrong, but he had also found a way to unbolt the door from the outside."

The baroness continued to keep silent, and in her eyes there was increasingly less surprise and increasingly more hate.

"The bolt is of iron, well maintained, well lubricated, and not very heavy. With a good magnet, you can actually move it from outside the door, which isn't very thick anyway. You just have to do it slowly and determinedly, and the bolt slides across. I tried it myself just a few minutes ago. And I managed it without any effort."

With much less effort at least than the effort it takes to stand here talking. The baroness lowered her head. "Get out of here."

"I'm sorry, Baronessa."

"Not as much as I am. Get out."

❧

Returning to the main door, he found Bacci, who, for once, had done what had been asked of him: apart from the reply, he had also brought with him the object of the reply, Jacopo Paglianti, son of Gerlando, stablehand to Barone Cesaroni.

Within half an hour, having given his officers the necessary instructions, the inspector had summoned all the residents to the drawing room (apart from Lapo, who was still in pain, and the baroness, who was still in her wheelchair) and had given a short speech, hoping that his nervousness was not too obvious.

"Ladies and gentlemen, I have finally gathered together all the elements I needed to bring this case to a conclusion. I am here, mainly, to apologise for the invasion to which you have all been subjected. In addition, I should like to explain to you in the most direct and honest way possible what happened this weekend, and what will be happening shortly."

Can words paralyse? Apparently yes.

"Allow me first of all to introduce Signor Jacopo Paglianti, assistant stableman to Barone Rodolfo Cesaroni di Canpetroso. Signor Paglianti, would you be so kind as to repeat what you told me and my assistant a little earlier?"

"Yes, of course, I'd be so kind. Last year, around Easter, this horse arrived, this Monte Santo. He was a fierce animal, all instinct, you couldn't hold him. It took me a long while to tame him.

But it was worth it. First—"

"Signor Paglianti, I'm sorry, could you go on to what happened last Monday?"

"Monday? On Monday I meet Teo, I mean poor Teodoro, and tell him, there's a horse running on Friday that's a real winner. Nobody knows him, I trained him very early in the morning. They're giving me fifteen to one. Think about it and let me know. And he goes, why should I think about it? If you tell me he's a sure thing, I'll put everything on him. I'll have enough to leave the castle and open my shop."

"His shop?"

"Yes, Teodoro wanted to open a tobacconist's shop, one of those posh ones, in Livorno. Anyway, he also tells me his girl is expecting, because he'd knocked her up, and getting married wouldn't be a bad thing, and this horse had come along just at the right time."

"Did you hear that, Baron?"

"Of course I heard it," said the baron severely. "I hope you're finally convinced that the father of Agatina's child was clearly poor Teodoro."

"Yes, I admit that. So, Signor Paglianti, you gave indications to Teodoro Banti about the horse Monte Santo, telling him the odds were high, and it was almost certain to win."

Paglinati looked at the inspector suspiciously. "That's what they told me . . ."

"Don't worry, Signor Paglianti, I'm not interested in gambling. What I want to clarify is that Teodoro knew what he was doing when he bet a considerable amount on that horse. You know something about that, don't you, Barone? You also bet on that horse."

The baron smiled bitterly. "Yes, I did," he said, avoiding looking at Signor Ciceri. "Teodoro told me about him, and I took advantage of the tip. But I didn't know that Teodoro had also bet money on him."

"Please forgive me, Barone, but I don't believe you."

"It's true, I assure you. I really had no idea. Teodoro often placed bets for me, but didn't usually tell me about his own."

"That's not what I meant, Barone. I don't believe you when you say you also bet on that horse."

And here the inspector's tone of voice changed noticeably. "The bookmaker clearly remembers receiving only one bet from Signor Teodoro Banti. And, besides, the idea that Teodoro could have placed two big bets on the same horse makes no sense. Signor Paglianti, would you be so kind as to explain why?"

"No, I . . . You said . . ."

"Signor Paglianti, please finish what you've started."

Cecilia had read only in books that there existed a tone that brooked no objection. Now, listening to the inspector, she realised that this kind of tone also existed in the real world.

"Alright, then. Teodoro had to place a big bet, because everybody knew he was betting for the baron. The baron often bet large sums of money on stupid horses, begging your pardon, Barone. I can't even bet, they won't accept my bets. It was important to bet quite a bit of money, otherwise people would suspect that Monte

163

Santo wasn't your average kind of horse, which was what they all thought."

"I understand. So it was easy for Teodoro to place his bet."

The baron coughed, like someone trying to appear composed. "I'm sorry, Ispettore," he interjected, "but this is madness. Teodoro worked for me. Why wouldn't he have told me about Monte Santo?"

"Because then you would also have bet on him. Two big bets simultaneously, not just one. That would have made the book-makers and the habitual gamblers suspicious, and would have brought down the odds on the horse. It was quite common for you to bet lots of money on horses considered terrible hacks, hoping for a miracle. But Teodoro rarely gambled. On the contrary. Isn't that so, Signor Paglianti?"

"That's right. He never gambled. What would he have gambled with?"

The baron did not lose his smile. "Ispettore, I don't think I understand. Could you explain to me then how the betting slip came to be in my possession?"

"Because you stole it from Teodoro's pocket after discovering that he was to collect a big win on Saturday morning. Teodoro had come to see you after he won and revealed his intention to leave your employment, explaining to you that he had won a lot of money, not realising that you are no longer as indifferent as you once were to the subject. Having got into a good deal of debt, you found it a not inconsiderable sum, especially this weekend when you were expecting someone who was going to hold you to account."

The inspector paused for breath. The last round was starting.

"Unaware of this fact and wanting to share his joy with you, Teodoro told you about his win. In so doing, he gave you the opportunity to get hold of the money you needed."

"I understand," said the baron, looking at the others in the room as if begging forgiveness for this poor madman. "So, when Teodoro came to see me, I nimbly picked his pocket. He noticed and decided to poison me, but being a little distracted he knocked back the very poison he had prepared for me. Signor Artusi, I'd ask you not to leave those detective stories of yours lying about in future. You see" – he gestured toward the inspector – "what damage too much imagination can do to a zealous spirit."

Artusi was looking now at the baron, now at the inspector. As were all the others, in fact, with the expressions of people who find themselves witnessing an encounter of major importance but of whose rules they are completely ignorant. A bit like finding oneself in the middle of the final of the world cricket championship.

"No, Barone, I don't think that's the way it happened," said the inspector. "I think you poisoned your own glass, knowing perfectly well that Teodoro usually finished off your port, and that you went down to the cellar during the night to steal the betting slip from the corpse."

A hit.

"Oh, that's what you think, is it?" replied the baron, his voice cracking. "And how, pray, would I have got into the cellar, given that the door was bolted?"

165

"Just as you did when you were little. Moving the iron bolt from its place with a magnet."

On the ropes.

"But this is madness! Who told you such nonsense? Another wretched stableman you picked up in the village?"

"No, Romualdo. It was I."

The baron turned like someone who has been told by the fireman that the house in flames up there on the hill is actually his. Just outside the room was the dowager baroness, framed clearly in the doorway like a painting: Whistler's mother, perhaps.

The baroness' words seemed to strip the baron of his noble title. With an angry look, he made one last vulgar, plebeian attempt to wriggle his way out. "You have no way of proving any of your assertions."

"For the moment, no, Barone. But, as you perhaps know, I consider that whoever used the chamber pot in Teodoro's room is responsible for the crime. And the contents of the pot, which are still preserved in my office, will be analysed. Tell me, Dottore, you prepare the drugs for the baron's dyspepsia, don't you? What exactly do you prescribe to your patient for that affliction?"

"Cocaine, Ispettore. A mixture extracted from the leaves of *Erythroxylum coca* in a ten per cent solution of ethyl alcohol. To be taken in extremely moderate quantities."

Before the readers start thinking that the inspector is about to arrest the doctor for drug-dealing, it may be useful to explain that the use of cocaine for therapeutic purposes was perfectly normal at the end of the nineteenth century, and that it was one of the remedies favoured by the nobility and the upper middle classes of Italy for curing the symptoms of stomachache. The so-called *Vin Mariani*, prepared by a Corsican pharmacist exactly as the doctor has explained, but with Bordeaux instead of the alcohol solution, numbered among its most convinced and enthusiastic admirers His Holiness Pope Leo XIII, who bestowed a gold medal on the producer and even agreed to appear on posters advertising the product. The fact that a pope should attach such importance to a remedy for indigestion may lead the more malicious among you to wonder if he really did suffer from it to that extent and, if so, why? But let's not wander off the subject: we were in the Maremma, so let's go back there.

The inspector nodded solemnly in response to the doctor's answer, and moved as much as he needed to in order to have the doctor's face directly in front of him, and the baron's face quite visible in a mirror above the writing desk. "So, Dottore," he said after a carefully timed pause, "you prescribe this somewhat characteristic remedy for dyspepsia. Tell me, are the active principles of this preparation found in urine?"

"Er, yes."

"And is it possible to verify their presence by a chemical process?"

"Yes, certainly."

The inspector studied the baron's face in the mirror, without turning to look at him directly.

"Have you ever prescribed these drugs to anyone other than the baron?"

"Er, no. No. Only to him."

Knockout.

The silence increased in density, while the inspector wondered how he was going to conduct the baron out of the room. He had done well, but he did not feel like declaring a person under arrest in the name of His Excellency the King when the king was not in the room. By way of compensation, though, the mother and children of the guilty party were.

"Barone . . ."

Nailed by a chamber pot. What an indignity.

Monday, towards sunset

The sun was slowly sinking towards the sea opposite the castle of Roccapendente.

If this had been a day like any other, the baron would have sat down on the terrace in front of his house to admire – and make sure his guests admired – that grandiose spectacle. Unfortunately, this was not a day like any other: the baron had been escorted off the premises by officers Ferretti and Bacci, and it was likely that from now on, if all went well, he would be seeing the sunset through prison bars.

The members of the family had remained in the drawing room, while Artusi, Ciceri and Ispettore Artistico had slipped out and were strolling in the garden.

"Well, now, Signor Artusi, I have to thank you."

"Indeed, Ispettore?"

"Very much so. When you mentioned your magnetic personality, and the need to keep it under lock and key, it was as if I had been slapped in the face."

And it was true. At these words, the inspector had been struck by a vision: that of young Romualdo Bonaiuti, not yet a baron, in short trousers, drawing a magical groove on the cellar door with a magnet, opening the door, and shutting himself inside, safe in his lair. He himself, when he was small, had built himself a secret refuge that was closed in a similar manner, with a small iron hook which slipped into an eye. To open the door, you had to know where the hook was and draw an arc with the precious magnet, which, together with a little knife, constituted his personal treasure.

"And now I also understand the cook's words."

"The words you mentioned to me this morning? The precious thing that Teodoro was keeping in his wallet. That, too, was of help to me."

"Precious thing?" asked Ciceri.

"Yes, the poor fellow talked about it on the day he died. And the cook, knowing that a photograph of Agatina had been found in his pocket, was really moved, thinking of the romance between Teodoro and his girl. But actually, Teodoro was referring to something quite different."

"Yes," replied Artusi. "Which now even I realise. The betting slip."

"Well, anyway," said Signor Ciceri, "this matter is no longer any concern of ours. Now that Ispettore Artistico has handed the guilty party over to the law, it's up to the judge. We can all go home. And justice will be done. Am I right, Ispettore?"

I'd gladly strangle you, said the look in Ispettore Artistico's eyes.

"No, Signor Ciceri. Justice will not be done. The law will be applied."

"Isn't that the same thing?"

"No. It's a profoundly different concept. If I could really dispense justice, I would force you to give back those ten thousand lire the baron gave you, and which did not belong to him. To all intents and purposes, that money was Signor Teodoro Banti's."

"Indeed? And how am I to give it back to him? Not an easy task, I'm sure you'll agree. And the dead don't even need money, as far as I know."

"The dead, no, but the living, yes. And Agatina is alive, even though guilty of attempted murder, just as the dead man's child will be alive and the legitimate heir of its father's property."

"I'm happy for the child, but it'll have to do without my money."

"Signor Ciceri, I ask you one last time: give back that money."

"And I reply, one last time, that the money is mine. You have no way to make me give it to anybody at all."

"Ispettore Artistico doesn't," said Artusi. "But I do."

❧

"Forgive me, Signor Ciceri," continued Artusi, while the inspector looked at him in amazement, "but at heart I'm still a merchant, and I think you have to give back that money, so that the dead man's unborn child can use it. It isn't yours."

"It's nice to see the two of you are in agreement. Unfortunately—"

"You're a photographer, Signor Ciceri. Tell me, in what kind of photographs do you specialise?"

Ciceri frowned. When someone changes the subject so abruptly, he is usually trying to take you by surprise. "Landscapes, mainly. But what pays best are portraits."

"What kind of portraits, if you don't mind my asking?"

"All kinds, whatever the customer desires."

"And what if the customer doesn't desire or isn't capable of imposing his own desire?"

"What is this all about?" the inspector cut in.

"I'll tell you what it's about, Ispettore. If you search through Signor Ciceri's personal effects, among the photographs he has developed you will find several that depict naked young people and children, of both sexes, in lascivious poses."

The inspector froze. The way in which he looked at Ciceri was not exactly friendly.

Unconcerned, Ciceri sustained his gaze. "They are artistic photographs. Anyone who understands a modicum about photography will be able to tell you that."

"That may well be. But I don't think the baron's estate manager, Signor Primo Amidei, is terribly interested in photography."

"What has the estate manager to do with it?"

"Oh, he has a lot to do with it, Ispettore. You see, some of these photographs are of his eldest son Cecco, and were taken on this very property. As you will remember, Signor Ciceri liked to have the boy go with him to see the most picturesque spots, and must have persuaded the young man in some way – with money, I assume – to indulge him in this hobby of his."

"And how do you know all this?"

"A little bird told me, Ispettore. But if you don't believe me . . ."

If the inspector had not believed him, it would have sufficed to look at Ciceri's face, which had literally turned white.

"Are you joking or what? Do you really plan to tell the estate manager?"

"What of it? Didn't you yourself tell me it's art? Perhaps he'll appreciate it."

"But . . . but if he sees . . . he'll kill me . . . he'll beat me to death."

"Yes, that's possible," said Artusi philosophically. "Even quite likely, I'd say."

"But . . . Ispettore!"

"Go on."

"I hope you will take steps. This is my life we're talking about. Wouldn't it be a crime if the estate manager beat me to death?"

"Of course it would. But let me reassure you. Should Amidei cause your death, or any permanent injury, it would be my duty to arrest him and make sure that the full force of the penal code is brought to bear against him. But until that happens, there's almost nothing I can do."

❦

About an hour had passed. The coachman had just taken away Ispettore Artistico, who bore with him the twelve thousand six hundred lire won by Teodoro, with which he intended to open an interest-yielding account in the name of Agatina and her unborn child, taking the cook as a trustee, which would allow the child to grow up in some comfort, even though it might have to do without its mother for a while. Not that this was a foregone conclusion: there was the question of honour, there was the fact that Agatina was beautiful and prosperous, and this, although it

173

shouldn't, would make an impression. At any rate, the inspector had done his job. Now it was up to the judge.

The most pitiful part of it had been telling Gaddo, the new potential master of Roccapendente, what would happen now.

When the inspector had finished his explanation, Gaddo had risen from his father's armchair and had looked at the inspector incredulously. "Are you serious?"

"Signorino Gaddo, do you really think I would joke about this?"

"No, of course not. Forgive me. So, by staining his hands with this . . . this . . . my father *de facto* loses his noble title. And the financial privileges linked to it, too."

"That is correct, Signorino Gaddo."

Gaddo stopped looking at the inspector. "In other words, I will pay for a sin committed by my father. I woke up this morning an heir and rich. In the course of the day, I find myself bourgeois and poor. Does that seem fair to you?"

Poverty, my friend, is not having enough to eat. And you won't have to deal with that just yet.

While the inspector was searching for a reply, he heard Gaddo continue, "Although it isn't true to say I'm entirely without blame. Like Lapo, I could have asked about the money, I could have asked why some objects were being sold. There were so many signs, now I realise it, but I just stayed quietly in my own world, writing poetry. I sinned by omission, and now I'm paying the price. With what, I don't know, but I'm paying. There is one big difficulty in all this."

"And what is that?"

"It's the fact, my dear Ispettore, that I don't know how to do a damned thing. Pardon my coarseness, but now I am about to become a plebeian and I will have to get used to it. I've never worked a day in my life, and even if I wanted to, I don't know how. Yesterday I was a poet and a future baron, today I'm an idiot who's good for nothing."

"You have a castle and many loyal servants."

"And with what am I to maintain these loyal servants? The walls of the castle can't be cooked and eaten."

"No, Signorino Gaddo. But they can house other people, who would be only too pleased to pay to stay here."

Gaddo looked at the inspector as if he had just been kicked in the head.

"You have greater assets than most people in the kingdom today. It won't be difficult for you to settle your father's debts with a small part of this property. After which, this place could become a high-class hotel."

"In other words, you're suggesting that I live by making other people pay to enter my house?"

"It's what your father was thinking of doing, you know."

"In the house where I grew up? I don't know if I'd be able to do that. You really—"

"Listen to me, Signor Gaddo, because I'm about to speak to you very sincerely. Where I come from, there are whole villages and parts of towns that are ruled by outlaws, who impose their own justice. *Camorristi*, we call them. In order to rule these little empires of theirs well, they have to keep them isolated, remote, difficult to reach and impossible to penetrate. And that is why what these people are actually ruling over is a heap of rubbish. These places are falling to pieces and have no future." The inspector rose to his feet, and smoothed his trousers. "Signorino Gaddo, you can be lord and master, without any title, of a castle which will become a pile of rubble, or you can be a citizen of an open world, which everyone can enter and which you can administer. The choice is yours. But at least you have a choice. There are people who don't have that choice, and never will."

❧

Now, only Artusi had yet to leave the castle. He was standing on the lawn with a large case, waiting for the coachman, his top hat in one hand and the basket with his cats in the other.

As he looked around, Artusi saw a familiar figure in the distance. Not knowing what to do, he put on his top hat, then took it off again. He was pleased to see Signorina Cecilia, but now might not be the time to appear too cheerful in the presence of someone whose father had just been arrested.

"Signorina Cecilia . . ."

"Signor Artusi . . ." said Cecilia, and then she paused. "Signor Artusi . . ."

"Go on, signorina."

"I want to thank you for what you did for Agatina. It was very noble of you."

"Thanks to you, signorina. Perhaps I shouldn't say this, but it was precisely your forays into the guests' luggage that provided me with the necessary information to persuade Signor Ciceri to relent."

"Really? Well, I'm glad. At least I've been of some use, haven't I?"

"Don't say that, signorina. You can be useful to many people."

"Do you think so?"

The silence lasted a few seconds. Then all at once Cecilia said, "Dottore Bertini told me I have a real talent for medicine."

And she blushed as she said this, as if ashamed to admit that the baron's departure might have dragged her out of her lethargy and had perhaps opened the doors to a genuine life.

"I agree. You're attentive, curious and methodical. If you also have a good memory, it's the perfect field for you."

Cecilia looked at him. "I have an excellent memory. And I'm about to demonstrate it."

"Really?"

"Really. You never answered my question, so I am obliged to ask it again. What exactly are *tommasei*?"

In the distance a cloud of dust appeared. The trap that would take Artusi to the staging post was coming. He smiled and turned.

"Alright, signorina. In Florence at the beginning of the century there was a famous literary club, founded by Vieusseux, who was from Geneva. This club numbered among its members the finest minds of our literature, including Niccolò Tommaseo, to whom we owe our basic dictionary of synonyms. Tommaseo, though, was not unanimously considered a man of great intellect, and among his fiercest detractors was the greatest poet of our century, Giacomo Leopardi."

Artusi smoothed his whiskers and continued.

"If you will allow me, signorina, I must use scurrilous language. As you may know, popularly, to insult someone and make it clear to those listening that he is not a very clever person, we say that that particular individual is breaking a very specific part of our body, a part which is essential for our reproduction, and which is usually only referred to in the plural, since nature" – here he cleared his throat – "supplies us not with one but a pair."

Artusi smiled.

"That is how a coarse, uncultivated man puts it. But Leopardi was a man of genius, and a poet. And that is why he often mocked his target metaphorically, referring to these delicate parts of the body by the name *tommasei*."

Cecilia started laughing.

And as she laughed, she felt like crying. But she stopped herself.

"Come and see me in Florence, signorina. You will be a very welcome guest."

"Without fail, Signor Artusi."

Epilogue

Florence, Saturday, 1 July, 1895

At last, after many attempts, I managed to make the pie I tasted during my strange visit to the castle of Roccapendente. I realised, after a few failures, that it is essential to add the ingredients in the right order, one at a time, and let each one cook as long as necessary, since each of the components of this pie demands time to acquire the right texture and the right taste.

It is also essential to use only the finest ingredients, but that is something that everyone who cooks knows: peppers do not exist as a platonic, unchangeable category, every pepper is different. But if we find a merchant we can trust, keep our eyes open, do not throw away the parts that have gone rotten but cut them off with a small knife, we can do a lot for very little.

But enough of this chatter, I sound like an old fool. I here transcribe the recipe, although I have decided I will make it only for myself and my guests, and will not include it in my book; I love to tell stories connected with each dish, and in this case there are so many I could tell, they would require a book by themselves.

Gypsy pie

2 yellow peppers; 3 spoonfuls of oil; 3 sticks of celery, 25 centimetres in length; 300 grams of bread from the day before; 2 decilitres of milk; 500 grams of tuna in oil; 100 grams of black olives; a few leaves of parsley; 2 eggs; 0.5 decilitres of the finest cream; 20 grams of butter; 40 grams of breadcrumbs

The dish would gain from the use of red olives.

Peel the peppers over a flame, rub them in straw paper, remove the seeds and cut them into small pieces. In a large pan, brown the celery, thinly sliced, and when it has turned brown add the pepper and cook for as long as it would take to greet a beautiful lady.

Meanwhile, put the bread to soak in the milk after bringing it to the boil.

Then add the tuna, after crumbling it with a fork, and let it sink in. Stirring constantly, add the stoned olives, the softened and kneaded bread, parsley, salt and pepper. Then let it cool.

Put the mixture in a bowl, soak the eggs in it, and wash it well with your hands; then thicken it with the cream.

Grease an aluminium dish and sprinkle it with half the breadcrumbs; then pour in the mixture, cover the surface with the rest of the breadcrumbs and cook it in the oven.

This should be enough for four people; even more, if they are satisfied with it.

More recipes from the kitchen of Pellegrino Artusi

Carciofi fritti
Deep-fried artichokes

This is such a simple dish that it seems hard to believe there are people who don't know how to make it. In some areas they boil the artichokes before frying them; this is wrong. Elsewhere they dip the artichokes in batter; quite apart from being superfluous, this masks the flavour of the vegetable. I prefer the method they use in Tuscany. Given that the Tuscans eat huge – even excessive – quantities of vegetables, they're better at cooking them than anyone else.

Take two artichokes, discard the tough outer leaves, trim the tips, remove the stems, and cut them in half. Even if the artichokes are not particularly large, cut each half into 4 or 5 wedges, giving you 8 to 10 pieces per artichoke. Refresh the pieces for a while in cold water (adding lemon juice will prevent the artichokes from discolouring). Then drain, but not too thoroughly, and immediately dip into the flour so it sticks to the artichoke pieces. Lightly beat the white of one egg, stir in the yolk, and salt the mixture. Shake any excess flour from the artichoke pieces, then dip them in the egg mixture and leave to sit briefly. Heat the oil, then add the artichoke pieces one by one to the pan. Remove when browned and serve with lemon wedges – as everyone knows, any deep-fried savoury dish is enhanced by a squeeze of lemon, and it brings on one's thirst.

❦

Maccheroni con le sarde alla Siciliana
Maccheroni with sardines, Sicilian style

For this recipe I am indebted to a spirited widow whose Sicilian
husband loved to cook the dishes of his native land.

> *600 grams fresh sardines*   *6 salted anchovies*
> *1 fennel bulb*   *Olive oil*
> *500 grams long Neapolitan maccheroni*
> *125 ml tomato sauce or 2 tablespoons tomato purée*

Remove the heads and tails from the sardines, cut in half length-
ways and fillet. Then flour the sardine halves and fry them. Salt well
and put to one side.

Boil the fennel, then drain and chop finely.

Cook the pasta, drain and put to one side.

Clean and fillet the anchovies, then fry them in plenty of olive
oil, breaking them up with a wooden spoon. Add the fennel, lightly
season with salt and pepper, stir in the tomato sauce or purée
diluted with water, and simmer for 10 minutes. In a heatproof dish
mix the pasta, sardines and sauce, allow to brown in an oven and
serve hot. Serves six or seven.

✦

Pollo alla cacciatora
Hunter's chicken

Chop a large onion and soak in cold water for at least half an hour,
then drain and fry in oil or lard. Put to one side when cooked. Joint
a chicken, brown the pieces in the remaining fat, then return the
fried onion to the pan. Season with salt and pepper, add a glass of
Sangiovese or other good-quality red wine and the same quantity of
tomato sauce. Simmer until the chicken is cooked through.

Warning: this dish is not suitable for weak stomachs.

Cignale fra due fuochi
Roast wild boar

First prepare the following marinade: bring 750ml of water and 125ml vinegar to the boil, add 3 or 4 finely chopped shallots, a couple of bay leaves, some parsley, and simmer for about 5 minutes, adding salt and pepper. When the marinade has cooled, pour over the boar and refrigerate.

Line the bottom of an ovenproof dish with 3 or 4 paper-thin slices of lardo (if you can find it) or pancetta. Pat the boar dry, season with salt and pepper, and put in the dish with a whole peeled onion, a bouquet garni, a knob of butter and, for a joint of about one kilogram in weight, 125ml of dry white wine. Cover the meat with more slices of lardo or pancetta, butter a sheet of baking paper and place on top of the joint. Put in a 180°C oven and roast the meat until tender, basting it occasionally with the cooking liquid to prevent it from drying out. Strain the liquid, spoon off as much fat as possible, and pour over the meat prior to serving.

~~~

Piccione a sorpresa
Pigeon surprise

This isn't much of a surprise, but it's a wonderful dish.

If you only have one pigeon to put on the spit and you want it to serve more than one person, you can stuff it with an appropriately sized veal steak. Pound the veal to tenderise it, season with salt, pepper and a pinch of mixed spices and dot it with a few small pieces of butter. Roll it up, place inside the bird and sew the cavity shut. Adding sliced truffles to the seasoning will make the end dish even better. You can also fry the pigeon's gizzard and liver separately in butter, pound them in a mortar and spread the resulting paste over the steak. This allows the flavours of the two types of meat to combine, improving the overall taste.

~☙~

Triglie col prosciutto
Red mullet with prosciutto

The saying "as mute as a fish" does not always ring true. On the contrary, red mullet, like the *ombrina* and a number of other fish, produce sounds when contracting the muscles that regulate the passage of air in their swim bladders.

The largest and tastiest mullet are caught off reefs. However, the medium-sized mullet that the people living on the Adriatic coast call *rossioli* or *barboni* will suffice for this recipe. Wash and clean 4 mullet, pat dry and lay in a shallow ovenproof dish, adding salt, pepper, 2 tablespoons of olive oil and 1 tablespoon of lemon juice. Let the fish sit in this marinade for several hours, turning them occasionally. Take 4 slices of prosciutto and trim them to the size of the mullet. Arrange a few sage leaves on the bottom of the dish, dip the mullet in breadcrumbs and put them in the dish, belly-down, sandwiching the slices of prosciutto between them. Sprinkle with a few more leaves of chopped sage, pour over the marinade and bake the fish, covered, in an oven preheated to 200°C.

To make the dish more elegant, before marinating remove the backbones by slitting open the bellies, opening up the fish and pressing them flat. Then close again.

~☙~

Baccalà Montebianco
Mont Blanc salt cod

How strange culinary terminology is! Why is this dish called "white mountain" rather than "yellow mountain", which is what it in fact looks like? And how did the French, with a giddying leap of the imagination, arrive with their name for this: *brandade de morue*? *Brandade* apparantly comes from *brander*: "to move, excite, brandish a sword, pike, lance, or similar weapon". Well, we don't use any weapons here, merely a simple wooden spoon. You have to admit that the French are highly inventive!

Still, this recipe warrants serious consideration, as salt cod prepared in this way is transformed from a basic ingredient into a dish refined enough for a banquet, either as a starter or a savoury.

½ kilo soaked baccalà   *250ml top quality olive oil*
125ml cream or milk

Remove all skin and bones from the salt cod, then grind in a mortar and put with the cream in a pan over a low heat, stirring constantly. When all the cream has been absorbed, add the oil drop by drop, as if you were making mayonnaise and keep stirring with your "weapon" – wooden spoon – to prevent the mixture from curdling. Take off the heat and allow to cool. Serve cold with thin slices of truffle, slices of toast, or caviar crostini. If you've prepared this dish correctly, the oil will not separate from the mixture.

Serves eight.

❧

Fagiuoli a guisa d'uccellini
Beans cooked like little birds

In the *trattorie* of Florence, beans cooked in this way are also called *uccelletto* style.

Boil half a kilogram of freshly shelled white beans and drain. Place several sage leaves in a pan, cover with 100ml of olive oil and heat. When the sage leaves start to blister, add the beans and season with salt and pepper. Cook until the oil has been absorbed, stirring occasionally, then add 100ml tomato sauce. When the sauce has been absorbed, the beans are ready to serve. Dried beans can also be prepared in this way after they have been boiled.

These beans can be eaten on their own or are an excellent accompaniment to boiled meat or sausages.

~~

Cavolfiore colla balsamella
Cauliflower in béchamel sauce

All cabbages, whether they be white, black, yellow or green, are the sons or stepsons of Eolus, the God of the winds, something that those who can't bear wind should be aware of. The plants are known as "crucifers" because their flowers have four petals in the shape of a cross.

Remove the leaves from a large cauliflower, make a deep X-shaped cut in the stalk, and boil in salted water until the florets are tender. Drain, cut the cauliflower into little pieces, and sauté in a pan with 2 tablespoons of butter, seasoning with salt and pepper. Transfer to an ovenproof dish, cover with grated parmesan and béchamel sauce, and put in a 200°C oven for 10 minutes, or place under the grill until the top is browned.

Serve the cauliflower as a savoury or, even better, with stewed meat or boiled chicken.

Cenci
Rags

240g flour	*2 eggs*
20g butter	*1 tablespoon brandy*
20g icing sugar	*A pinch of salt*

Combine all the ingredients into a fairly stiff dough and knead thoroughly, adding flour if the dough is too sticky. Sprinkle with flour and cover, then allow to rest. Roll out the dough to a thickness of around 3mm, and cut with a knife or pastry wheel into strips two fingers wide and a palm's length. Twist and crinkle the strips, fry in hot oil or lard, then allow to cool before dusting with icing sugar. This recipe will make a large bowlful. If the dough forms a crust while resting, knead again before rolling out.

❧

Budino di limone
Lemon pudding

1 large garden lemon	*6 eggs, yolks and whites separated*
170g sugar	*1 teaspoon rum or cognac*
170g cups sweet almonds, plus 3 bitter almonds	

Simmer the lemon whole for 2 hours, pat dry and taste. If the lemon is bitter, soak in water until the bitterness has leached out. Pass the lemon through a sieve. Add the sugar, almonds – peeled and ground to a fine powder – the 6 egg yolks and the cognac or rum. Mix well. Whip the whites and fold them into the mixture. Transfer the mixture to a mould that has been greased and lined with bread-crumbs. Bake in an oven at 170°C for half an hour. This pudding can be served either hot or chilled.

❧

AUTHOR'S NOTE

It's no coincidence

Sometimes, when reading a book, we wonder whether the author has chosen a detail (a particular name, a specific year, etc.) for a definite reason, or whether that detail has been put there by chance.

It has to be admitted that recognising a deeper meaning in an apparently random detail gives us a wonderful feeling; in a word, it gratifies us. It makes us feel alert, cultured, collaborative: we have deciphered the author's secret code, and not everyone can do that.

Sometimes, though, this feeling is disrupted by a background noise: the possibility that everything has been invented. Perhaps that character is called what he is because the author thought it sounded good, that's all. That is why, without explaining more than I have to, and giving those who have ears to hear the satisfaction they deserve, it seems to me only right to specify which details have not been chosen at random.

❦

The book takes place in 1895, and that is no coincidence. It was a year when a certain number of rather significant events took place. On December 8, Guglielmo Marconi succeeded in sending the first radio signal over a hill, and the rifle shot with which his butler signalled that the transmission had arrived was one of the few cases of a firearm determining the course of history without anyone being killed. That same year, the Lumière brothers held the first public demonstration of a contraption called the "cinematograph" in Paris on December 28, Maria Montessori became the first woman to be admitted to the Società Lancisiana (the association of Roman doctors and teachers of medicine) and Pellegrino Artusi published the second edition of his *Science in the Kitchen and the Art of Eating Well*, complete with a hundred new recipes, ranging from doughnuts to Neapolitan macaroni.

In a word, the world was changing. It was becoming a more open place, a place where it was possible to communicate more easily, and in which certain forms of discrimination were starting to show their senselessness thanks to the inspired madness of a number of pioneers.

The noble protagonist of this novel has the title of baron, and that is no coincidence either; without enlarging too much on this, nowadays this title is used in a very specific context, to refer to a certain kind of person and their use of public institutions.

The most alert and erudite readers will have recognised the book that Cecilia reads aloud to her grandmother: *The Emperor's Tomb* by Joseph Roth. That was no random choice either, even though it involves taking some liberties with historical reality.

Finally, the pie that goes through the whole book is a gypsy recipe: and as you will by now have guessed, that is no coincidence either.

ACKNOWLEDGEMENTS

This book would never have seen the light of day without the passion, care and sincerity of Antonio Sellerio, who approved of the plot when I told it to him, and suggested I set it in Tuscany, not in England as I had originally planned.

In the same way, this book would never have occurred to me if as a young university student I had not wasted time when I should have been studying reading the exhilarating revival of *Il Libro Cuore (forse)* by Federico Maria Sardelli and the learned but still hilarious *Novissimo Borzacchini Universale* by Ettore Borzacchini. I am indebted to both these authors, and in the book there are two explicit tributes to their brilliant humour.

I thank Piergiorgio, Pierino, Ciccio, Valeria for giving me, when I went to live on my own, a copy of *Science in the Kitchen and the Art of Eating Well*, and Pino and Leonora Rossi for helping me to appreciate the culinary and literary contents of the book. I thank Maurizio Vento for lending me the autobiography of Pellegrino Artusi: one day I'll give it back, but not yet.

I thank Laura Caponi, Cinzia Chiappe, Christian Pomelli, Mimmo Tripoli and my wife's mother Liana for preventing me from making too many blunders.

I thank my friends, who have read, examined, criticised and exhorted: Virgilio, Serena, Letizia, Rino, my fellow citizens of Olmo Marmorito (with an honourable mention to Sara, the only one to send me notes on time) and all those I have forgotten.

Last but not least, that I was able to start writing again after a year's silence is thanks to the patience of Liana, Gianna, Salvina, Giovanna, Gino and Tina, who have nursed and fed little Leonardo; and thanks to Samantha, who apart from pampering the little man of the house has also taken care of the big one and his manuscript. Without her, neither would have got anywhere.

MARCO MALVALDI

MARCO MALVALDI was born in Pisa in 1974, and is both a crime novelist and a chemist. His first novels made up the Bar Lume series set on the Tuscan coast, and he has since published *Argento Vivo*, which was a number one bestseller in Italy in 2013. For *The Art of Killing Well* he was awarded both the Isola d'Elba Award and the Castiglioncello Prize.

HOWARD CURTIS is a translator from Italian, French and Spanish, most recently of novels by Jean-Claude Izzo, Gianrico Carofiglio and Luis Sepúlveda. He has won several awards, and his translations have twice been nominated for the *Independent* Foreign Fiction Prize.